LIBBY SCOTT & REBECCA WESTCOTT

DO

FIND YOUR

YOU

KNOW

FIND

ME?

YOURSELF

SCHOLASTIC

Published in the UK by Scholastic Children's Books, 2020
Euston House, 24 Eversholt Street, London, NW1 1DB, UK
A division of Scholastic Limited.

London – New York – Toronto – Sydney – Auckland
Mexico City – New Delhi – Hong Kong

ISBN 978 0702 30095 0

A CIP catalogue record for this book is available from the British Library.

Printed by CPI Group (UK) Ltd, Croydon, CR0 4YY
Papers used by Scholastic Children's Books are made
from wood grown in sustainable forests.

1 3 5 7 9 10 8 6 4 2

www.scholastic.co.uk

To my dear and very loved Charlie, thank you for being the best dog in the world and the inspiration for Rupert. Since I was a baby you were by my side, loving and protecting me. I don't know what I would have done without you. Although you couldn't talk you could listen, and just having you there for all those years was the best feeling in the world. I will never stop missing you, but your soul will stay in my heart forever and I know I will meet you one day at the rainbow bridge. Please wait there for me. This book is dedicated to your memory.

XOXO Libby

To Zachary, Georgia and Reuben. Three fierce kids who always stand up for what is right, no matter how hard that may be.

Rebecca XXX

CHAPTER 1

Can you see her? No? Then you're going to have to peer a little closer. You're going to have to try a little harder. Not that she's difficult to find. She's right there in front of you – you just have to look. It'll probably help if you listen too. Stop talking for a moment and put all the things that you *think* you know to one side.

Tally Olivia Adams is one hundred per cent unique. And if you want to get to know her then you're going to have to try seeing things from her perspective, which is only fair, really. She's spent the last eleven (almost twelve) years trying to fit in and see things from other people's points of view.

Take a few steps forward and put your hands on the side of the ladder. If you climb carefully, remembering not to step on the rotten third rung, then you can scale

1

your way to the top of the garden shed. That's where you'll find Tally, bent over her notebook with the early summer sun shining down on her head. It's getting pretty warm up here but Tally has work to do, and when she has her mind set on a task, nothing can get in her way. She's tenacious like that – which is probably another word that describes you, since you've taken the time to clamber up here and perch on the roof next to her.

She writes something down on the page and then looks up, chewing on the end of her pencil. The notebook is filled with words and sentences and diagrams, and after spending the last ninety minutes since she got home from school considering the situation and completing her assessments, Tally is fairly sure that she has got it figured out. The only thing left to do is to tell him, and she isn't relishing this task, not one little bit. There's no way to know how he's going to react and Tally dislikes surprises.

But she really wants to understand him better, and in her opinion it is always better to *know*. So she tucks the notebook under her arm, slides down from the ridge of the shed and climbs down the ladder to where he is waiting. He always waits for Tally, no matter where she is or what she's doing.

Tally pats his head and they make their way up the

garden and into the house. This kind of conversation is always better with a biscuit. Actually, Tally knows that most conversations are better with a biscuit.

"I've noticed you struggling with a few things," Tally begins, offering him a treat and then sinking down next to him on the sofa. "So I've been trying to come up with a way to help you. I'll talk you through it because it's important that you understand how I came to this conclusion. When this happened to me I really, really wanted to know *everything*."

He stares at her but remains silent, which she takes as permission to continue. Flipping open her notebook, Tally reads from the first page.

"Firstly, I looked at the way you communicate with others. You're very good at letting *me* know how you're feeling but honestly, I don't think that anyone else has a clue about what's going on with you and that's mostly because you don't show them."

She glances across at him and gives him a big smile. "I'm not saying this to be unkind, OK? It's all right if you don't want to share what's in your head. That's not a rule or anything."

She returns to the notebook, turning the page to the second point.

"You hate any change in your routine, don't you? Even if I've warned you that it's going to happen, you still get all shaky and scared and that makes you act in a bit of a silly way, sometimes."

He shifts on the sofa so that he's pressed right up against her leg. Tally is his safe place, just like he is hers, and he doesn't mind what she says as long as she always comes back to him.

"And lastly, there's the whole issue around your food." This time Tally lowers the notebook and stares him sternly in the eye. "I understand, I really do. But refusing to eat just because your breakfast is in a different bowl really isn't OK."

He returns her look and she relents, giving him a quick grin. "Yes, I know that I have a special plate and bowl and cup, but it's not like I'm going to let myself starve if I can't have them, is it? And I agree that food doesn't taste right if it's in the wrong bowl, but we still have to eat. That's a non-negotiable and if you want to stay here then you're going to have to cope with it, no matter how wobbly it makes you feel inside."

Tally closes the notebook. "So. After all that, what I'm trying to say is that you and I seem to struggle with the same things, which means there's a chance that you're autistic."

She pauses, waiting for his reaction. She really hopes he isn't unhappy about it – she can't stand it when people talk about autism like it's a disease or something *bad*.

Rupert stares up at her and then nudges his nose into her hand, which is what he always does when he's happy. Tally laughs and throws her arm around him.

"Yes! You're just like me! And now we can make things a bit easier for you. Like, I can tell Mum to buy two bowls for you so that if one gets broken then we've got a spare. And I'll make sure that I tell you at the start of every day if something different is going to be happening."

Nell walks into the kitchen just as Tally finishes speaking. Her thumbs are speeding across her phone screen, but when she sees Tally she stops tapping and shoves the phone into her back pocket.

"Who are you talking to?" she asks, heading across to the freezer. "And do you want an ice lolly? It's scorching hot today."

"Yes, please." Tally gives her sister a smile. Nell is nearly fifteen and she acts like she knows everything in the entire universe. But Tally knows that when they're at school, Nell is watching out for her. "Can I have strawberry? And I was just telling Rupert what I've worked out about him."

"Oh yeah?" Nell pulls two lollies from the freezer and

hands one to Tally. "And are we now the proud owners of the only special needs dog in town?"

Tally glares at her. "That's a bit mean," she tells her sister. "It's not very clever either. Rupert *is* a very special dog, but he doesn't have any more needs than you do, actually. His needs are just different."

Nell's face wrinkles. "Sorry. I wasn't trying to be unkind. Rupert is totally special, aren't you, boy? He's the best dog ever."

Tally can remember a time when Nell thought that Rupert, with his three legs and scruffy hair, was a huge embarrassment, and she opens her mouth to remind her, but then she closes it again. Mum says that people change all the time and that if someone is trying to be better then it isn't very fair to keep bringing up their past mistakes. It doesn't mean that Tally can't log it in her memory though, just in case Nell gets super-annoying at another time and needs bringing down a peg or two.

"Rupert is autistic," Tally tells her. "I've considered the evidence."

Nell frowns. "Can dogs even *be* autistic?" she asks. "How can you tell?"

"Well no, not *really*," Tally admits. "Only people can be autistic. But being autistic means seeing the world in a different way – and I *know* that Rupert doesn't see things in the same way as other dogs."

Nell nods slowly. "That's true. Rupert isn't like any other dog that I've ever met."

Tally grins triumphantly. "I told you. He's autistic. And now he knows, so he doesn't have to feel worried about being different or not fitting in. Now he can find his tribe."

Nell laughs, but it isn't a nasty laugh so Tally lets it go. "And who are his tribe?" she asks. "Where is he supposed to find them?"

Tally stands up and Rupert instantly leaps to the floor on his strong three legs to join her.

"He's already found them," she says. "I'm his tribe."

Nell smiles and crouches to pull Rupert into a hug.

"I like the sound of having your own tribe," she says, looking up at Tally. "I wish I had one."

Tally frowns. "You have," she tells Nell. "You've got loads of people who understand you and get how you're feeling. You've got a *massive* tribe. Me and Rupert have only got each other."

Nell looks concerned. "You told Mum and Dad that things were getting better at school this term. And you're good friends with Aleksandra, aren't you?"

It's true. Aleksandra is an excellent friend and when

they're together they always have a good time. Aleksandra loves drama lessons as much as Tally does and she's always got a smile on her face. Plus, she's got the best laugh that Tally has ever heard and it's completely infectious – once she gets going it's almost impossible not to find yourself laughing along with her.

But not everything about school is better. She still has to see Layla, Lucy and Ayesha every day, and each time it's a reminder of what happened last year when her so-called best friends betrayed her. Even though she's worked really hard to get over it, it still hurts. And school is still school.

Not that Nell would understand about that. She can't. She doesn't know what it's like to walk down the corridors feeling awkward and self-conscious and like everyone is looking at you, even when you know that they probably aren't. Nell has got lots of friends to hang out with, not just one person. Aleksandra is Tally's one friend, but Tally isn't Aleksandra's only friend, she knows that. And it's hard to feel OK about your one, single friend when she's got a whole load of other people to talk to and have fun with, no matter how much of a great friend she might be to Tally.

But it's all going to be OK because she's got Rupert

and even though he's a dog, he gets it. He *knows* her and as long as she's got him then she'll never be on her own.

Date: Wednesday 3rd June.

Situation: Just hanging out after school.

Anxiety rating: 4. There's nothing big to worry about but there's still two days of school to go and anything could happen – I know that from experience.

Dear Diary,

Well, here we are, you've made it back for more of my thoughts. Congrats. Now let's get on with the diary.

It's great to be here again, writing in my journal, lying with my feet up against the headboard of my bed, which is my favourite writing position. Sorry I've not written in a while but I've been sooooo busy. Mum finally let me get a mobile phone but then seemed to instantly regret it as she thinks I spend far too much time on there. To be honest, I know I do, but the lure of a notification is just too much to resist. It's like it's calling me and won't let me rest until I've seen what is being posted in the group chat. I can easily spend an entire evening getting involved in some kind of "pointless conversation" as Mum calls it. Mum insists I can only keep my phone if she checks through it each night when I'm in bed – and I hate that she does that. It feels like I'm not just talking to my friends but to my mum at the same time. I hate grown ups' rules.

My mum won't let me read *her* messages so I don't see why she gets to read mine. To be honest, I think it's just nosiness on her part. Maybe she doesn't get interesting enough messages from her friends.

So, talking of friends, it's been a jumbled start to the summer term at Kingswood Academy. Things at school have definitely settled a bit since the Horrendous Tiger Mask Incident of the autumn term. Luke is still annoying but not nearly as nasty as he was before. We just tend to keep our distance from each other. Same with Lucy and Ayesha – I've shuffled away from them. It's not that I hate them, I just don't think they are perfect friends for me, and I do like things to be perfect. You are probably wondering about Layla. Layla, who was my best friend all through primary, but somehow just wasn't brave enough to stick up for me when others were making my life a misery. Yes, that really hurt at the time, but to be honest, *I'm* wondering about her too. I sometimes wonder if I was a bit hard on her, as although she let me down when I needed her the most, she'd still been a good friend over the years. I'm just not 100% sure if I can trust her again. But I guess not everyone is perfect 24/7, every second, every day. Well, except me of course. JOKING!

Yeah – so Layla and me, who knows what will occur

there? The person who is actually now the closest to me is Aleksandra. She's really kind and chilled and I think she understands me. Though let's not jump in there too soon. Nell (my annoying big sister) once said I could wind up the Dalai Lama if he caught me on an anxious day. (This joke only works if you know who the Dalai Lama is and I didn't and I bet you don't either and think we are talking about shaggy animals.) Anyway, Aleksandra seems to like me and she laughs at my jokes, which is a huge point in her favour.

I bet you are wondering what happened to the tiger mask I used to hide behind whenever things felt like they were too much for me to face? That mask was also a great friend to me. It offered me safety and a sense of calm whenever I put it on. But I took a real knock when the others at school got hold of it one day and used it to mock me. My heart immediately starts racing whenever I think back to that awful day, when I went into full-on melt-down in front of the whole class. I suppose I've kind of managed to cope without it, though it's still on my mind and I do sometimes wear it in my darkest times. Some-times when I'm in a difficult situation I get an urge too strong to resist. And then I wear it again. Just for a short while, in my bedroom. It still gives me a good feeling. But most of the time it remains in the same place on top of the wardrobe in my room. Like a friend waiting for you to message them for support when you need them.

It's kind of good that since Layla told everyone about my autism, following the terrible tiger mask day, I no longer have to pretend not to be autistic. I don't mean I used to go up to people and say, "Hi, I'm Tally and I'm not autistic," but I definitely hid it from people. Now I talk about it a bit more and the other kids ask me quite a bit about it. I always tell them that this is just how it is for me – I don't speak for all autistic people because just like snowflakes we are all different, but we have some similarities too.

I mainly explain to them that for me, autism means I FEEL things in a different way to others. Everything feels more intense for me than it seems to for other people who I know. Noises, lights, pain. But most especially emotions. All this means I get anxious more quickly than others might. It's just how it is. And that anxiety usually comes out as anger, especially at home. At school I used to mask all that completely. Now I'm learning to be myself and let it out a bit more. The only thing is, people tell you to be yourself, but really they mean "just be yourself when you are feeling happy or excited". When you're feeling scared or angry or worried or miserable they're not so keen. It's a debate I am always having with myself. My favourite slogan at the moment is "Be yourself, but not too much!" If I ever get to be a famous author I shall sign that inside all the copies of my book along with my name. Lol, Tally Adams, maker of motivational mottoes. I could do Christmas crackers too, and fortune cookies. And posters for school corridors. Urgh, school.

Talking of school, Mrs Jarman is still the teacher at school who understands me best. She's created a Safe Space for me, next to the library. It's somewhere I can go when I get overwhelmed and just need to get away from it all and Mrs Jarman let me write a list of the things I wanted in there:

Music – the sort I listen to when I go to bed – kind of soothing, or sound effects like rain or the sea.

Lights – fairy lights, the yellow, warm kind.

Cushions – especially furry ones or those two-way sequins that you can brush up one way or another. They feel amazing. Unless they are those cheap, stiff ones.

Tent – I like to be able to lie with my head in the tent.

YouTube clips – of waves or a forest in the rain being projected on to a screen, so I can imagine I'm somewhere calm.

Sensory toys – Fidget spinners, squishies, slime, anything that feels good.

Books and magazines – to flick through.

Neutral tones – schools seem to think all kids love bright colours. Well guess what? You're wrong. Bright colours sometimes make my head hurt. Unless they are sweets like Haribos, of course.

Candles – Mrs Jarman said I couldn't have real ones but she got some battery-operated flickering ones, which are great because they are voice activated and go on or off when I shout at them (the librarian next door must have a great time listening to me attempting to get the candles on).

She asked me if I wanted some plants in there as well but I said no in case they had insects on them. And even if they

15

didn't, I couldn't relax with them there because I would be worrying about it.

I've also found another space where I feel really relaxed and safe and that is the school library. The smell of the books is comforting and as good as a new car/new shoe kind of smell.

I like flicking through the pages of books although I'm still waiting to find a book with a character like me in it. Maybe one day any autistic girl will be able to walk into a library and see herself in a book. I can picture it now – the main character will be just like me and when she reads the book she will suddenly feel like she's not alone. That would be brilliant.

Anyway, Miss Clementine, (pronounced "Clem-en-teen" which is obviously wrong, but I let it go and haven't corrected her) the school librarian, seems to have taken me under her wing. She loves books so much that she is making me love them too. She is very clever in how she does it: she doesn't encourage me too much, or *tell* me to read something (like my dad does). She just says, "It's completely your choice, but I loved this book," and leaves it on the counter and says, "If you don't want to take it now you could try it another time." So the library is another safe space for me and Miss Clementine helps me with my homework sometimes too. Homework is just the worst and it puts me under so much stress. If I can't sleep at school then why should I do work at home? Homework is an unnecessary evil. Honestly, how does doing a word-search in French make me better at speaking French? And if you want me to learn facts about plant colonization then just tell me them, instead of giving me a complicated webpage where I have to find the facts myself. My brain doesn't work well at picking that stuff out.

Anyway, don't get me started on that – let's think about good things.

Rupert. The best thing ever – he's waiting for me to take him for a walk right now so gotta dash. Catch you later.

CHAPTER 2

"I'm asleep." Tally keeps her eyes closed, even though she knows it's pointless. "Go away."

Footsteps cross the room and then she hears the swish of her curtains as Mum pulls them open. Frowning, Tally burrows under the duvet and pulls it tightly around herself, imagining that she's a human burrito.

"It's gone ten o'clock," says Mum, in a chirpy voice. "We had an agreement, remember? You can have a lie-in but then you have to get up. We've got lots to do today, Tally. Come on, rise and shine!"

"I'm not ready," Tally murmurs, her voice muffled by the duvet. "Come back in half an hour."

It's not entirely the truth. You can only wake up if you've actually been asleep and Tally has barely slept a wink all night. Mum should know better than to try and make her get up because she knows exactly how many hours Tally was awake. If there's one thing that Tally hates more than waiting for a big day to arrive, it's being the only person awake in the house at night. It makes her feel scared and alone, like she's the only girl in the entire universe.

The mattress dips as Mum sits down. Gently she peels the duvet off Tally's face.

"Come on, sweetheart," she says, trying to stifle a yawn. "It's a beautiful day outside and we're going to have lots of fun. Everything is organized and you know the whole plan for the day. There's absolutely nothing to worry about."

That's easy for Mum to say. Tally *is* worried and the worry is making it hard to hear any of the words that are coming out of Mum's mouth. The worry is taking Mum's words and messing them up, so that everything she says just makes it worse. The words jumble together and twist themselves around until they're a horrible prediction of the day to come.

Have to get up.

Lots to do.

Organized.

Worry.

"You're going to have a really fun day," Mum repeats with a big smile.

It's too much.

"I am *not* going to have a fun day," shouts Tally, throwing the duvet off and flinging herself out of bed. "Not now you've told me that I am. I can't just *have fun* because everyone thinks that I should, you know? And now I'm going to feel really bad if I don't have *enough* fun, because you're all expecting me to have a great time and it's going to be all my fault if the day is rubbish."

She pauses to take a deep breath and swings her legs off the bed. Mum doesn't move. Her hands are clasped tightly together as she watches Tally pace around the room, her arms flapping and stimming at her side.

"So really, it's better if I just stay in bed all day and you can get on with your plans and then nobody is going to get upset or disappointed."

Tally sinks on to a chair and focuses on a felt-tip stain on the carpet. Maybe if she stares at if for long enough then Mum will get the message and leave her alone.

"I'm sorry, Tally." Mum's voice is quiet. "I didn't mean to make you feel hurt or upset. Nobody wants you to have to do anything that you don't want to do." She pauses and Tally glances up through her eyelashes. "You can have a completely fun-free day if you want to. It's your day so it's your choice. OK?"

She smiles at Tally and stands up.

"I'm going to go downstairs now. You can choose whether you'd like to join us in the kitchen or you can go back to bed if you'd prefer to do that. It's completely up to you – no rush."

Mum walks out of the bedroom and leaves Tally alone, which is all she ever wanted in the first place. She didn't ask Mum to wake her up and she didn't ask for a great big fuss. Now she can go back to sleep and everything will be fine.

Except that now the room feels wrong. Tally looks around, trying to find the source of the problem. Maybe it's the sun shining in through the curtains? She stands up and pulls them tightly closed, but the wrong feeling won't go away, so she reaches for Billy, her favourite cuddly toy, and squeezes him tightly.

But even Billy can't make her feel better.

Tally starts to hum her tune, the one she made up that always helps when something isn't right. But it doesn't help. Not when she knows that she can stay in her room for as long as she likes but today isn't going away. There's only one thing to do and that is to get on with it and hope that nothing goes wrong like it usually does.

Standing up, Tally plods slowly out of the room and goes downstairs, still in her pyjamas. When she pushes open the kitchen door she can see Mum, Dad and Nell sitting together at the table and Rupert lying in his bed by the back door. The table is groaning with gifts, all wrapped up in shiny birthday wrapping paper.

She can do this. Just as long as they all remember the rules and don't say the words. It's supposed to be her day, after all, and she can't possibly have a good time if everyone is telling her that she has to be happy every five minutes.

"Can I have some orange juice, please?" she asks. "And a piece of toast?"

Dad gets up. "We've got some crumpets in the cupboard," he tells her. "Would you like one, as a treat?"

Tally nods her head but she doesn't sit down. It's been a while since Mum and Dad made her eat her meals at the kitchen table with the rest of them and she usually takes her food into the living room or up to her room where she can sit quietly and eat in peace. But today is different. Today is important, and while she's terrified about it going wrong, she doesn't really want to be on her own either. She wants to feel special and it's tricky to feel special when nobody is paying you any attention.

She pulls out a chair and sits down, trying to ignore the surprised look that Mum shoots across at Dad. She's just sitting down to eat breakfast. It's not a big deal or anything.

Nell pushes the pile of presents towards her.

"You've got tons of gifts, Tally! Open mine – it's really brilliant!"

Tally looks down at her juice and swallows hard. She knows that Nell doesn't mean to be bossy, but this is why she hates birthdays so much. Everyone is always ordering you about and telling you what to do.

Open this present.

Blow out the candles.

Eat the cake.

Have a fun day.

Tally loves presents and candles and cake, and she really, really enjoys having fun. Her dream birthday has all of those things – but when *she* wants them, not when other people decide that she should.

"I chose it myself," Nell continues, pushing her gift closer to Tally. "And I paid for it with my own money, so you'd better like it!"

Her voice is jokey but Tally knows that there is nothing funny about being given a present that you don't like.

23

It's the opposite of funny, actually – people get very upset if you tell them that the hideous and extremely scratchy cardigan that they gave you for Christmas is the worst gift that you've ever received. Auntie Sheila got upset, anyway.

Tally grits her teeth and locks the squirmy, anxious feeling away in a box in her head where it will stay until later. And then she looks up at Nell and forces a big, happy smile on to her face.

She can do this. She knows the script.

"Thank you very much," she says, taking hold of the parcel. "I wonder what it can be?"

Other people always seem to say this, even though it seems to Tally like a ridiculous waste of time, effort and words. You don't have to wonder. You can just unwrap the gift and find out. But they don't like it if you just rip the paper off everything and don't keep up a constant dialogue about what you're doing. They seem to think you're not being appreciative enough or something.

Nell laughs. "You'll never guess! Seriously, you could try for a whole year and you'd never get it right!"

Tally scowls. If she was daft enough to sit here and try to guess what the gift could be for three hundred and sixty-five days then she's fairly sure that she could probably figure it out. Nell says the most ridiculous things sometimes and it irritates Tally deeply. She puts her hand on the parcel, intending on pushing it back across the table, but then she catches sight of Nell's excited face and she can't do it. Nell would be hurt and Tally never, ever wants to make anyone feel that way, no matter how annoying they might be. And she can see that Nell has at least bothered to wrap it just the way that Tally likes. She must have remembered last year when Tally turned eleven and Mum wrapped the present with too much sellotape. It took forever for Tally to open it and in the end she had to rip the paper off, which was too loud and meant that the paper had to go in the bin which she really, really hated because 1) it's bad for the planet and 2) she'd intended on reusing the wrapping when it was Rupert's birthday. There wasn't much of her birthday left after the meltdown had finally ended.

Slowly and very, very carefully, she pulls on a small piece of tape and folds back the paper, trying not to rip it. She can feel the gaze of three pairs of eyes boring into her, watching her every move. She makes sure that her mouth is arranged in a giant smile so that Nell will know that she likes the gift.

But once the paper is removed, there is no gift. Instead, there is a cardboard box that feels heavy, just like Tally's heart.

She can't go through all of that again, she just can't.

"Hurry up!" urges Nell, leaning towards her, and Tally resists the urge to throw the box on the floor and run back to the safety of her bedroom.

"Nell." There is a warning tone in Mum's voice. "Let Tally open it at her own speed."

Nell makes a little huffing sound but she sits back in her chair. Tally breathes out, a long, deep breath that helps her tummy to stop swirling and then she looks across at Mum.

"You can finish opening it later," Mum tells her. "It's your birthday all day and there's no rule that says presents have to be opened at breakfast time." She pauses for a second and gives Tally a reassuring smile. "I've always thought it would be nice to have gifts to open later on in the day. Or even tomorrow."

Tally shakes her head quickly, trying to make the buzzing sensation go away. She loves getting presents but at the same time, it's just too much.

"I never asked you to give me a present," she murmurs under her breath, but everyone goes very still and she knows that she's done what she always does.

She's messed up her birthday yet again.

"I can open it," says Nell, her voice quiet. "You know, if you want me to? It's for your room anyway, so I could set it up for you."

The buzzing inside Tally's head drops as she gives Nell a grateful look.

"That would be good," she says. "Thank you."

Nell reaches for the box and stands up. "Come on then. I can't wait to show you what it is!"

She looks down at Tally expectantly, clearly hoping for some kind of a reaction. Although possibly not the reaction that she'll get if she keeps on pushing. Tally can feel herself teetering on the edge of a meltdown and the way that her big sister is smiling at her makes Tally want to either scream and lash out or run away and hide – she knows that Nell wants her to play some kind of game where she pretends that everything is great but she isn't a puppet – she can't just perform in a certain way because everyone expects her to.

Tally bites down the words that are trying to force themselves out between her lips. They are words that will tell Nell exactly what she thinks of her demands and Tally doesn't really want to say them. She sometimes wishes that there was a safe place you could keep unkind words that your mouth wants to shout but your brain knows that it shouldn't, because *not* saying them once they've been thought always makes her feel squirmy and uncomfortable.

"I'll come up in a minute," she tells her sister, attempting to ignore the slightly hurt look on Nell's face. She knows she's not being very fair but it's the only way to stop herself spiraling into the meltdown that she can feel hovering around the edges of her brain.

Nell shoots Mum a quick glance and Tally sees Mum give her a nod and half a smile. She knows what that means.

Keep Tally happy.

Don't react to her.

If this were any other day she'd be furious but she's too worried about the presents to do anything except give a huge sigh of annoyance. Nell stomps out into the hall and Tally hears her marching upstairs.

"You should think about going with her," says Dad, taking a slurp of tea. "I think you're going to like her gift."

Tally eyes the rest of the presents. If she goes with Nell now then they're just going to sit here, waiting for her. She won't be able to relax, knowing that she's got to open them all up and give the correct reaction to each and every one of them.

"These gifts are all from us," Mum tells her. "They aren't wrapped up inside the bags so you can have a quick peek if you like. Then you'll know what they are and you can look at them properly later, whenever you feel like it."

Tally's shoulders slump in relief. She's been let out of birthday-prison and now that she knows there's no horrible unwrapping to be done, she's curious to see inside the gift bags. Leaning forwards, she spies a book that she's been wanting to read for ages and a game for her console and a couple of new squishies that she'll have to try out later to check that they have the right kind of squishiness. And then she looks into the last bag and sees something that she doesn't want to leave until later.

"I like this," she says quietly, pulling it out and turning it over in her hands. "I really, really like this."

Mum and Dad smile at each other.

"Well, you're a writer now," Dad says. "And every writer needs a good notebook to record their thoughts."

"I've almost filled up the journal that you gave me last year." Tally keeps looking at the notebook, running her finger along the wavy, tiger stripes. "This one is perfect."

"That's exactly what we thought," agrees Dad.

"Thank you." Tally puts the book down and moves around the table to stand in between her parents. She bends down and reaches out her arms so that she can give them both a hug. "This is not a bad birthday. So far."

"High praise, indeed!" says Mum, giving her arm a squeeze. "Now I think your sister is probably blowing a fuse upstairs, waiting to show you her gift. Do you think you can help her out and pop up there for a minute before we have a major incident on our hands?"

Tally nods and picks up the notebook. "I'll go and calm her down," she assures Mum. "She gets super-moody if she's kept waiting. I thought she'd be better now that she's fifteen but if anything, she's getting worse."

"That's teenagers for you," says Dad, nodding in agreement. "We should make the most of your last year as a rational human being before you turn thirteen."

Tally spins round and fixes him with a look.

"I'm not going to get moody just because I'll be an age with a *teen* in the number," she tells him. "That's ridiculous. If I'm moody it's going to be for an *actual* reason, OK?"

"I'll do my best to remember that," he says, his mouth twitching at the corners. Tally stares at him suspiciously in case he's about to laugh at her, but he makes his face serious again so she lets it go.

"We aren't going to the pizza place until teatime,"

says Mum. "Aleksandra is meeting us there so you've got plenty of time to get ready."

Tally glances at the clock. She's looking forward to seeing her friend but the idea of having to put her nice clothes on and leave the house on time makes her heart start to pound.

"Is it too late to stay at home and order pizza?" she asks, her voice quiet. "I know I said I wanted to go out but maybe Aleksandra can come here instead?"

Mum smiles. "It's your day. We can do whatever you want to do and you don't have to decide now."

"Tally!" Nell's voice drifts down the stairs. "Your present is ready!"

"I'll choose later," Tally says. "After I've seen Nell's gift." And she heads out of the kitchen and upstairs, her tiger notebook clutched firmly in her hands.

Nell is standing outside Tally's bedroom door and if Tally didn't know any better then she would definitely say that Nell looks nervous.

"I've set it all up," Nell tells her. "Will you let me cover your eyes when you walk into the room?"

Tally scowls. It's supposed to be *her* special day so why is Nell asking her to do something else that she totally hates? Her big sister is really pushing her luck today.

"Please," adds Nell. "I mean, you don't have to but it'll make it so much better if you close your eyes."

"I suppose so," moans Tally, thinking that if there was a brilliant-and-giving-little-sister-of-the-year award, she should absolutely be nominated. "But if you let me walk into any walls then I'm going to be furious and my birthday will be ruined."

"I won't let you walk into anything," promises Nell, putting her hands over Tally's eyes. "Just take a few steps forward and then I'll let you look."

Tally puts one foot in front of the other and wonders what can be so important that Nell would go to all this bother. Whatever was inside that cardboard box must be pretty special.

"One more step," murmurs Nell. "OK – you can look now!"

Tally opens her eyes. The first thing she notices is that her blackout blind is pulled down and the room is in darkness. Almost darkness, anyway. The second thing she notices is the object sitting on her bedside table, and she moves towards it, unable to tear her eyes away.

"Do you like it?" asks Nell. "Do you?"

Tally barely hears Nell's voice. She sinks down on to her bed, puts down her notebook and gazes at the gift, captivated by the colours and the swirls and the feeling of calm that is flooding through her body.

"What is it?" she whispers. "It's beautiful."

"It's a bubble lamp," Nell explains, sitting down next to her on the bed. "As soon as I saw it in the shop I knew that you'd love it. Have you seen the jellyfish? They almost look real!"

Tally leans against her sister but doesn't move her eyes away from the lamp. Inside, jellyfish float and drift and the colours make her feel as if she's at the bottom of the sea, with nothing to bother her and nothing to worry about.

"Thank you," she murmurs.

Nell puts her arm around Tally and pulls her in for a hug. "I'm so, so glad that you like it."

"I love it," Tally tells her. "It's the best present that I've ever had in my whole, entire life and you are the best big sister that I've ever had."

"You do know that's not much of a compliment, don't you?" snorts Nell. "You've only got me."

"I know," agrees Tally. "And sometimes you are incredibly hard work. But I'm glad that I've got you."

"I'm glad I've got you, too," Nell tells her. "Which is lucky, cos I think we're stuck with each other for life."

Tally laughs. There are worse people to be stuck with than Nell.

Maybe this birthday isn't going to be as tricky as she thought it would be.

Date: Saturday 6th June.

Situation: my twelfth birthday.

Anxiety rating: 8. Birthdays are very, very anxious days. I feel excited and stressed and worried and like I want to have all the attention on me but at the same time I don't want anyone making me feel like I have to do something in a particular way.

Dear Diary,

Let's talk about birthdays. We all have them. Dangerous candles, sickly cake, crowded house, but worst of all that stupid song. You know, that "happy birthday to you" song that everyone is obsessed with. Grow up, people! Now on the good side, the presents almost outweigh all the bad parts. And there are a lot of bad parts. Like when everyone is huddled round you like penguins as you peel back the wrapping paper and the pressure burns through you like fire. And when you have to pretend that you like something that you HATE. Like when Auntie Sheila gave me that itchy cardigan that felt like sandpaper against my skin and everyone told me to try it on. Also, my mum always tells me to say I love it when I don't but she also tells me never to lie so make your mind up.

Good points about birthdays: Presents. Presents. Presents.

Bad points about birthdays: Presents. Yes, presents can be a mixed blessing. Sometimes it can stress me out not knowing what's inside the giftwrap. Some people probably love surprises but I have mixed feelings about them. Once, when I was little, I peeled back all the wrapping before my birthday and then had no surprises on the actual day, which was really disappointing. But if someone else knows something I don't then it makes me feel like they have all the power. But a really good surprise is something that you don't know is coming like the day my go-kart arrived in the garden when I was nine.

I only ever pick one or two people to come to my party as too many people make it overcrowded and it stresses me out. Once I had loads of people, and that was awful as all the attention went off the fact that it was my birthday and went on to the fact that there were loads of people crowding out my house and touching my stuff.

For the last five years a man with reptiles has come to my house for my birthday treat. He brings loads of boa constrictors and lets them out for us to cuddle. But first he gives us a talk on them (the same one every time, but it never gets boring). I really like the man because he seems to get so interested in his snakes. They are the most important thing to him and he knows everything about them. I can relate to that. It's a bit like me and Taylor Swift. He also has a beard with beads in it, which I really like but my mum says she wants to chop off with a pair of scissors. She was annoyed with me for telling him that but she shouldn't have said it if she didn't mean it, should she? Anyway, his love of snakes is so infectious that you can't help loving them too. Snakes get a bit misunderstood – people assume they are unpleasant and cold and uninterested, but when you get to know snakes you find out that they are incredibly friendly, majestic creatures who absolutely love a cuddle as long as they are in the right mood. The last time the reptile man came he had a reptile girlfriend too. She isn't half lizard or something, I just mean she loves them just as much as he does and they work together telling people amazing facts about their reptiles. They don't seem to think the other one is weird for loving snakes and lizards so much, and I like that. Maybe one day I'll meet someone who loves Taylor Swift as much as I do and we can talk about her together for the rest of our lives.

Anyway, the other thing I find hard about birthdays is people arriving at the house and all the demands, like answering the door and saying goodbye – two of my pet hates. I hate greetings. They are so awkward and I never know what to say. I have tried rehearsing my greeting but it always comes out wrong and then I have to face the mortification of knowing the other person is thinking about it for the entire party. Saying goodbye is also awful so I usually stay up in my room and then mum gets all narky about it. People seem to find these things so important and I don't know why. Surely what's important is the good time you have with people when they are here, not making a big deal of how well you say hello or goodbye to them?

So that is a bit of my thinking about why birthdays and autism don't mix that well, for me anyway. The funny thing is I still always look forward to my birthday coming. And that's how PDA* (or demand anxiety as I prefer to call it) gets you. You can be really excited about doing something and then it sneaks up on you out of nowhere and kind of grabs the great opportunity straight from you, without any choice on your part. I want to just relax and have fun like others do on special occasions like this. But all it takes is for me to feel slightly under pressure and like I *have* to do something and that's it. Not only can I not go ahead with the thing, even if it's something I'm desperate to do, but my anxiety will go so high that it will probably start coming out in anger too and then I really start upsetting those around me. This anxiety means I also want to control everything too – I want to know exactly what is going to be happening. So I usually start asking how many presents I'm going to be getting, will it be more than last year or the same and so on. This of course means I come across like I'm some kind of ungrateful, greedy kid. Nell once said I was behaving like Dudley Dursley, the awful, spoilt brat character out of Harry Potter. That really hurt, firstly because no one wants to be compared to Dudley Dursley, and secondly, because this is not something I'm choosing to do, PLEASE TRY AND GET THAT PEOPLE! I'm getting a tiny bit better at recognizing what's happening to me at these times, but I haven't yet got very much better at controlling it. To be honest it can seem to come out of nowhere, though there will always be something triggering it, no matter how small it might seem. This means my mood can go from really happy to being furious in a matter of seconds. Which must be awful for my family. Well, it's not exactly a bundle of laughs for me either.

Of course, even though all the above will be going on for me, I will be doing my very best to cover it all up in front of anyone but my very closest family. Yes, dear diary readers, I still continue to mask a lot the behaviours I hate the most, to hide them from most people because, well, because no one wants their worst bits to be on show for everyone, do they? But now that most people know that I'm autistic I do find I can be a little more open about how I'm feeling and what's bothering me, which definitely helps a bit.

*PDA stands for Pathological Demand Avoidance. The best way of describing it simply is to say that it means we just cannot cope with everyday demands and expectations as they make us feel so anxious. This anxiety also makes us feel the need to try and control everything. You can imagine how hard this makes things for us, especially with friendships and home and everything at school.

CHAPTER 3

Aleksandra is waiting at the school gates, glancing anxiously at her watch and shuffling her feet. There isn't very much that fazes Aleksandra, but she gets really, really worried about time, and Tally is constantly trying to explain to her that they don't need to arrive everywhere ten minutes early.

"You're late," she tells Tally. "We've got year seven assembly this morning, remember? Come on – we're going to have to hurry."

Tally grimaces. She's getting used to being at Kingswood Academy but there are still some things that she hates and assembly is one of them. Everyone crammed together in the hall, people surrounding her on every side. It feels hot and close and she always has to work really hard not to feel like she's about to be crushed to death by sweaty year seven kids. She always tries to go on the end of the line, partly to avoid feeling suffocated, but also because she's worried about needing to go to the bathroom. Having to try and get out of the hall without anyone knowing that she needs to use the toilet is the most awful, mortifying thing in the world. She doesn't like being late for things either but she'd happily make an exception for assembly.

Today's assembly is going to be worse than normal because Mr Kennedy is going to be giving them the final details about the trip next week. And Tally doesn't want to hear a single thing about next week. Not one thing. She went on the year five residential trip when she was back in primary school. That didn't exactly end well *and* it was only one night, not five.

"I can't wait to find out what our activities are going to be!" says Aleksandra, giving Tally a big grin. "I heard that we get to do climbing and kayaking and all kinds of amazing stuff!"

"I might not go," mutters Tally, scuffing her feet on the tarmac as they walk towards the main entrance. "It sounds stupid to me."

Aleksandra stops and spins to face Tally, the smile dropping from her face.

"You *have* to go," she implores. "It's going to be brilliant fun and it won't be the same if you're not there."

Tally scowls. "I don't have to do anything. Neither do you. You could stay here with me if you want to."

Aleksandra shakes her head and starts walking again. Tally pauses for a second and then dashes to catch up with her. She might not want to go to assembly but she wants a detention for being late even less.

"I've *got* to go," Aleksandra tells her as they climb the steps. "My mum has been saving up for months to pay for it. She'd be really upset if I backed out now. Anyway, it's going to be fantastic. I'm really looking forward to it!"

Tally thinks about this as they join the throng of kids heading into the hall. She hasn't given much thought to how much the trip to GoCamp might be costing Mum and Dad, but she does know that Mum has been into school and had several meetings with Mrs Jarman. Mrs Jarman took her out of PE last week to show her a load of pictures on the website so that Tally could get an idea about what to expect. It was supposed to help her feel more relaxed about the trip but instead it's given her nightmares about being dangled off a cliff or being forced to kayak in the sea. The *actual* sea, with waves (probably) and sharks (possibly) and freezing cold water (definitely).

"Please say you'll come," pleads Aleksandra, weaving her way through a particularly slow group of kids. "I know I won't have anywhere near as much fun if you're not there too."

"Everybody settle down!" booms Mr Kennedy from the front of the hall. "Anyone not in a seat in the next twenty seconds can expect to be on litter-picking duty at lunchtime."

There's a scramble as people rush to sit down. Tally freezes as someone pushes past her, jabbing her in the back with their elbow. Somebody else barges into her and she can feel her heart beginning to pound. And then Aleksandra reaches across and puts a reassuring hand on her arm.

"It's OK," she says. "I've got us two seats right here." She pulls Tally down to a chair and Tally's heart rate starts to return to something like normal. She's safe with Aleksandra. Aleksandra is her friend and she understands. She didn't even mind going over to Tally's house instead of the pizza restaurant on Tally's birthday, even though she told Tally last week that she never got to eat out and was really excited about it.

"I'll go on the trip," she whispers. "But only because I'm an excellent friend and I know it won't be much fun for you without me, OK?"

The huge beam that spreads across Aleksandra's face makes Tally's tummy feel warm inside.

Mr Kennedy gestures to one of the teachers who are standing at the side of the room and the lights dim, before the huge screen at the back of the stage lights up with the GoCamp logo.

Mrs Jarman steps forward and addresses the hall.

"So, as you all know, next week we're taking the whole of year seven on an adventure of a lifetime," she starts.

"Yay! An entire week of chilling out!" yells a boy from the back of the room and the hall erupts into laughter. Mrs Jarman waits for the noise to die down and then shoots a stern look towards where the voice came from.

"If you think that the purpose of this trip is to *chill out*, then you are sadly mistaken," she informs the room. "You might not be in school next week but believe me when I tell you that you *will* be learning."

A groan spreads around the hall and she raises her hand. "You'll be learning the kind of things that it's impossible to learn in the classroom," she continues. "You'll be learning to take responsibility, not just for yourselves but for others too. You'll be learning to face your fears. You'll discover that strength and courage come in many forms, and most of all, you'll learn that you are capable of doing far more than you ever thought you could."

The hall is silent now. Mrs Jarman presses a button on the remote control and a montage of pictures is displayed on the screen behind her. Tally has seen them already, but they seem even more frightening the second time around. She stares as photographs of kids doing terrifying things appear in front of her eyes, with titles that scream "danger" at her. Rock climbing and gorge scrambling and vertical challenge, not to mention high ropes and night orienteering and raft building.

"I don't know how I'm going to be brave enough to go across those ropes," whispers Aleksandra, giving Tally's hand a quick squeeze. "But it does look kind of amazing, doesn't it?"

Tally nods, unable to reply.

She really, really hopes that she isn't making a giant mistake.

At the end of assembly, Mrs Jarman tells them all to return to their tutor rooms.

"The regular timetable will start again for lesson two," she explains. "Lesson one is going to be spent arranging the accommodation for GoCamp. There are a lot of you to organize, so we're sorting that out in tutor groups. Your tutor will talk you through the different accommodation types and tell you how to put your preferences down. You can also write down the name of one friend that you'd like to be with. However, I must remind you that you won't all get your first choice or be with your friend, so be prepared for that."

Tally turns to Aleksandra. "What are you going to—" she begins, but then Mr Kennedy starts yelling at everyone to leave the hall in a calm and orderly manner and her words are drowned out.

Not that it matters. Tally already knows that there are two choices of accommodation – tents or cabins. There's no way that she would ever choose to sleep in a horrid, cold, damp tent, and she's sure that Aleksandra will feel the same way.

She'll ask to stay in a cabin and put Aleksandra's name down as her one chosen friend. And then they can do everything together and have loads of fun and Tally won't have to worry.

It's all going to be completely fine.

Date: Monday 8th June.

Situation: Assembly about the school residential trip.

Anxiety rating: 7 and a half. I'm very worried about going away for a week but Mrs Jarman has been helping me and I know that I'll have Aleksandra with me, which is a very good thing.

Dear Diary,

Today we had an assembly about camp. To me this trip sounds like utter hell – yet everyone else is excited about it. We go next week and all the worries are flying around in my head like fireworks: what if I get homesick? What if Rupert dies whilst I'm away? What if my whole family die? The worries made my stomach flip like when I go on the ghost train, but in a very bad way. One whole week without my mum, dad, sister, dog and most of my teddies. It's all too much! How to make an autistic person feel anxious – take every single one of their safe and secure rituals away and tell them it will be an adventure of a lifetime.

My mum sent me on a worry workshop that a friend of hers, Elizabeth, was running. I learnt that if I have a worry at any time, I can jot it down but then I have to leave going over it until the Worry Window. The Worry

Window is for twenty minutes each day (I have mine at 5 p.m. – 5.20 p.m.) and it's where I can go over my list of worries and really think about them, and see which ones I can do something about and which I can't. Stopping after twenty minutes was really hard at first as it was like an extra demand on me, but then I started needing less time for my Worry Window. At the moment though, I'm feeling totally overwhelmed with worries and finding it hard to stick to twenty minutes. But here goes anyway – this is a list of my worries about going to camp:

1. The worst thing is that I can't take my phone, and my phone is a kind of friend to me. It is something I can escape into when I've had enough socializing. Watching YouTube videos of Taylor Swift totally relaxes me, and it's part of my chill-out ritual when I first get in from school. How will I manage without it?

2. No one else will be on their phones either, which means we will have NOTHING to do!

3. Getting dressed and undressed. In everyday life no one would be expected to strip off to their underwear and get changed in front of people they hardly know,

and yet schoolkids are expected to do that. I find PE bad enough, let alone having to get dressed from scratch in front of others. Maybe it was OK at age six, but we are twelve now and it's just not appropriate.

4. Falling asleep. I will NEVER get to sleep in a strange place like that and it will be even worse because I can't take Billy to help me fall asleep. He might get lost or laughed at or stolen.

5. Sleeping is also quite a private and personal thing – the idea of doing it in a room full of people I don't know that well, who might watch me while I'm asleep, is just creepy. Do the teachers all sleep together in one room, I wonder? I bet they don't, so why do they expect us to?

6. I find it weird just lying there next to someone trying to go to sleep. The awkward silence makes me really uncomfortable, so to prevent it I won't be able to stop myself from chattering all night and then I'll get into trouble from the teachers just like I did on the overnight camp in year five. In order to try and stop myself from talking, I'll probably have to stim. Stimming is

any kind of behaviour that I do when I'm stressed or excited. It makes me feel calm. It might be flapping my hands, or making certain sounds. The stimming I most often do in bed is picking at my toes, the nails and the skin around them. Mum hates me doing it as she says I will give myself ingrown toenails which will be really painful and I might even end up having to have an operation on them. So you see, school camp could end with me being hospitalized. Then I could pick up a terrible virus and die. All because of going on school camp.

7. Camp also means bugs: moths, flies, spiders, mosquitoes. Now, I love all creatures when they are outside where they belong. I even don't mind them in the house if I have brought them in myself. I remember one time I collected an ice-cream tub full of snails from the garden and brought them in to the warm because I felt sorry for them. You should've heard Mum shrieking when she discovered them sliding all over her kitchen cupboards. She used a lot of words too explicit to be repeated in the diary of a twelve-year-old. I love bugs generally, but they are not welcome when they are invading my space unin-

vited. I get stuck in a huge dilemma because I can't possibly harm or kill them, but can't sleep with fear of them crawling over me in the night, so I just lie there riddled with fear.

8. Eating. At school I have packed lunch cos there's only certain things I like, and I like those certain things a certain way. What's wrong with that? But at camp I'll have to eat whatever is provided and it won't be made just how I like it. Then everyone will notice when I try and make it edible, like in year five camp when I picked all the disgusting kidney beans out of the chilli con carne. How to ruin a good chilli con carne – stick a load of tiny little alien textures in the middle of it that you have to spend the whole time picking through! But even worse is the fact that EVERYONE feels they have the right to comment on what and how you eat. I am still haunted by the memory of everyone around the campfire laughing at my plate of meticulously sorted leftover beans. It makes me go hot just thinking about it. I can't bear the idea of being chilli-shamed like that ever again. And chilli is ALWAYS on the menu for anything like camping. Ugh.

9. OK, I've distracted myself from that worry by thinking of another. Having to get up first thing in the morning and immediately be sociable with others, and even worse, sit and eat breakfast next to them. At home Mum has finally stopped forcing me to come down and eat breakfast at the kitchen table. It was probably getting the cream cheese bagel on her head that did it, which I still feel bad about. Anyway, her or Dad bring me breakfast in bed every day, not cos I'm lazy but because I need time to get myself ready to face the world, with no forced conversation. At home everyone knows not to talk to me too much in the morning, but at camp I will have to be chatty from the minute I wake up until I go to sleep. This is going to be like some kind of torture.

10. Talking of torture, all this and then we have to do a ton of awful activities. I've been researching the activities online and they look terrifying. The safety harnesses could snap. The wooden poles you have to climb up might have rotted over the winter, and just as I get to the top they could splinter and send me crashing to a muddy and mortifying death. At least I won't have to eat chilli con carne then, I suppose. (JOKING!)

11. So I've just realized what my biggest fear about all this is. Camp is going to be full of demands – be here at this time, eat at this time, go to sleep at this time. Random adults will be shouting instructions at me all the time, I just know it – it will send my demand anxiety through the roof. How will I prevent myself having a great big massive meltdown in front of everyone again? The thought of this is just the worst.

Going to camp is one of those things that I really would like to achieve because I know it COULD be a fun trip. But all these fears are getting in the way. It feels like a vacuum cleaner has sucked up all the fun stuff and all I'm left with is these lumps of dirt that are too big to get hoovered up. I know I need to break them down somehow so they can get sucked away too. In the worry workshop, Elizabeth taught me that you have to work out if it's a worry you can do something about, and if it is then you have to work out what it is you can do. If it isn't, then you have to think about how likely that thing is to happen (usually very unlikely) and then try to distract your mind from thinking about it by doing something different. I like playing on my keyboard, or hanging out with Rupert or having a long bath, or listening to Taylor Swift or my new favourite girl band, Little Mix.

Well, that's my twenty minutes up, so I will have to think about all this tomorrow. I'm off to walk Rupert.

CHAPTER 4

The first lesson on Thursday morning is drama. Tally looks forward to it all week. As far as she's concerned, drama is the absolute best part of school, even if she does have to see Lucy and Ayesha. In drama, you can be anybody that you want to be. She's been trying not to hide her real self as much this term, but it's not always easy to trust that people won't laugh if she does something that they think is unusual or different. Sometimes she feels like she's putting on an act when she's at school, and it's hard work to squash down the parts of her that other people won't understand – like the stimming and flapping of her hands if she gets excited or the fear and anxiety if people keep telling her what to do and making demands on her that she just can't meet. She has to be a whole different type of Tally who is more like everyone else, and quite honestly, it's pretty exhausting.

At least in drama, *everybody* is pretending.

Mrs Jarman strides into the room, shooting Tally an enquiring glance as she passes. Tally gives her a quick thumbs-up – her special signal to let her teacher know that today is a good day. Mrs Jarman smiles and nods back at her before heading across to her desk.

"OK, let's have everybody sitting on the floor. We're going to start today's lesson with a new game called *"What I'm Really Thinking"* and I'm going to need four volunteers. Two of you will act out a scenario decided by the class and the other two will voice the thoughts of those people."

"I don't get it," says Ayesha. "How's it supposed to work?"

Mrs Jarman looks around the class. "It's probably easiest to show you. Who's prepared to go first?"

Half the class raises their hands. Things have changed a lot since the first few weeks of starting year seven, and most people have become more confident. Not that Tally always thinks this is a good thing. There are a few kids in year seven who could do with being a little less self-assured, as far as she's concerned.

"Let's see." Mrs Jarman wrinkles her nose, which Tally knows means that she is thinking. "Let's have Lucy and

Luke to act out the scene. Ameet – you can tell us what Luke is really thinking, and Tally, you can be the voice for Lucy's real thoughts. So – what situation shall we give them?"

"Going to the zoo!"

"Getting detention!"

"Meeting at a café!"

Voices ring out and Mrs Jarman raises her hand to quiet the class.

"All excellent suggestions," she says. "I think I like the last one best though – meeting at a café."

Tally smiles at Aleksandra, who is beaming with pleasure at having her idea chosen.

"The four of you come up to the front," Mrs Jarman continues, pulling a small table into the middle of the space. "Ayesha – can you bring me a couple of chairs, please? Now, let's imagine that Lucy is already at the café and Luke walks in."

She points to one of the chairs and Lucy sits down at the table.

"Any one of you can shout *freeze* whenever you want to hear what the characters are truly thinking," Mrs Jarman tells them. She turns to where Tally and Ameet are standing. "That's where you come in. Perhaps Lucy and Luke are saying one thing but thinking something quite different? It's up to you to decide."

Tally grins. *Of course* the things that they are thinking will be different to the things that they are saying! She spends most of the time trying to remember not to say the thoughts that are in her head. This is the *perfect* game for her, and she's pretty sure that she's going to be excellent at it.

"OK, let's make a start." Mrs Jarman moves to the side of the room. "Take it away, Luke."

Luke looks slightly unsure for a second, but then he straightens his shoulders and marches up to where Lucy is sitting.

"Hi, Lucy," he says, his voice brisk. "What's going on?"

"Nothing much," replies Lucy, tossing her long hair in the air. "How about you?"

"Freeze!" yells one of the boys and Tally looks at Mrs Jarman, suddenly unsure about what to do next.

"Tell us what Lucy is thinking right now," says the teacher. "What's on her mind?"

Tally looks at the scene. Lucy is lounging back in the chair, looking relaxed and chilled out, as if nothing could possibly be bothering her. Luke, on the other hand, is shifting from foot to foot and looking as if he might bolt from the room at any second. Somebody else might say that Lucy is bored and couldn't care less about Luke talking to her, but somebody else would be wrong. Tally knows that how a person is acting on the outside has got absolutely nothing to do with what they're feeling on the inside.

"She's nervous," she tells Mrs Jarman, who shakes her head.

"Tell us Lucy's thoughts," she explains. "Speak in the first person, as if you're inside her head. Let's start again from the beginning."

Luke makes a huffing noise but repeats his question.

"Hi, Lucy. What's going on?"

Lucy rolls her eyes and slumps even further in her seat. "Nothing much. How about you?"

"Freeze!" yells the boy again.

Tally is ready this time. She steps forward and looks at Lucy.

"Why is he asking me that question? There's *obviously* nothing going on. I'm just sitting here minding my own business. I wish people would stop wasting my time with stupid questions, just because they haven't got anything else to say."

She steps back and looks anxiously at Mrs Jarman, who

nods and then gestures to the others. "Good. Continue with the action."

"I'm fine," replies Luke. "Just thought I'd get a coffee."

"Freeze!"

Ameet smirks at Luke. "I hate coffee. If I ever go to a café I have a hot chocolate, but I can't really tell Lucy that, can I? I'll look like a right baby! Guess I'll just have to drink the gross coffee now. Great."

The class laughs and Luke glares at Ameet, who grins back at him.

"Can I sit down here?" Luke asks, clearly keen to move on.

Lucy shrugs. "If you have to."

"Freeze!" yells Aleksandra and Tally moves forward.

"Oh no. Why does he want to sit at my table? This is so embarrassing. What does my hair look like? And why did I decide to wear these old clothes today? I really liked Luke last year, but we haven't really talked much this term. What if he likes me? I don't even know if I still want to go out with him. Why is it all so confusing and weird?"

There is a moment of silence and then the class erupts. The sound bounces off the walls and even Luke has a grin pulling at the edges of his mouth. Tally smiles as everyone bursts into peals of laughter. Everyone except Lucy, that is, who is glowering fiercely at Tally.

"OK, that's enough!" Mrs Jarman holds her hand in the air again. "Let's all settle down, please."

"Can we keep going?" begs Ameet, his eyes sparkling in a way that makes Tally wonder what *he* might be thinking. "It's too funny, Miss! Please can we carry on?"

"No way." Lucy stands up. "It's stupid and I don't want to do it any more."

"You're just worried that Tally can read your mind and is going to tell us all how you really feel about Luke!" yells Jamie, causing a fresh round of laughter.

Tally doesn't join in this time, though. Instead, she's looking at the rapidly reddening face of Lucy and wondering if she might have done something wrong. She wasn't trying to make Lucy feel bad, she really wasn't. It was just that the way Lucy was flicking her hair and slouching in the chair made it obvious that she was only pretending to be relaxed when she was clearly feeling stressed. Tally does it all the time, so she knows.

"I think we're ready for a new task," Mrs Jarman tells them. "Get into groups of six and find a space."

Tally starts to head across the room to where Aleksandra is waving at her, but before she can reach her friend, Lucy moves in front of her.

"I suppose you think you're clever?" The words hiss quietly out of Lucy's mouth and nobody hears them but Tally. "Saying all that stuff about me liking Luke."

Tally takes a step back and stares at her. There's been an uneasy truce between her and the other girls since everything that happened with the tiger mask in the autumn term. She sits on the same table as them in science and sometimes joins in with their conversations, but it's not the same as it used to be. It can't ever be the same, not when Tally can't trust them any more.

"You don't have to be clever to tell the truth," says Tally. "In fact, if you think about it, you have to be super clever to *lie* because you have to remember all the things you've said that aren't true and the best way to do *that* is to convince yourself that what you're saying *is* true, which really means that you're lying to yourself." She pauses to take a breath. "And only a very clever person can do that."

"What are you on about?" Lucy is clearly not impressed with Tally's opinion. "You just made me look really stupid in front of everyone, saying that I like Luke."

Tally frowns. "Well, I'm really sorry about that. But you *did* like Luke last year – you went on and on about him all the time when we started in year seven."

Lucy rolls her eyes and Tally grits her teeth. She knows

what that look means – she's seen it often enough and it always makes her blood boil. If it were Nell who was rolling her eyes right now then Tally would be making her pay – but luckily for Lucy, Tally knows that she can't react like she usually would. Not at school.

"People change, Tally." Lucy spits the last word out, as if it's leaving a nasty taste in her mouth. "Just because I might have liked him last summer for about three seconds doesn't mean that I like him *now*. And it doesn't make it OK for you to tell everyone that I liked him before. Not when I told you that I was only pretending to like him in the first place."

"Get into groups of six, please," calls Mrs Jarman. Lucy gives Tally a last glare and storms off to where Ayesha is waiting for her.

Tally thinks back to the last time she had a proper conversation with Lucy and the others. They were standing in her kitchen, telling her that they were sorry for stealing her precious tiger mask from her bag and giving it to Luke – and then admitting that they'd told everyone that she is autistic.

It hurt more than she could ever tell them that they'd done that. Not the tiger mask so much, but the *telling*. Mum always says that everyone has a story and that it's up to each individual to choose how much of their story they want to share. Being autistic is part of Tally's story, and it should have been *her* decision to tell everyone. She's thought about it lots over the last few months and talked to Rupert about it too. He agrees with her. She isn't that bothered that everyone knows about the autism – what really annoys her is that someone else told her story and she's pretty sure they didn't tell it right.

Across the room, Lucy and Ayesha are huddled together, deep in conversation. Tally's tummy lurches, like it does when she's on a rollercoaster only not in a good way. She knows that they're talking about her. And maybe she shouldn't have said those things about Lucy liking Luke, because it's true, Lucy *did* admit that day in the kitchen that she was only pretending because she thought that it might make year seven a bit easier if every-one thought she was more grown-up. Maybe she should say sorry again?

But then Ayesha glances up and gives her a snarky look, and any thought of apologizing rushes out of Tally's head. They didn't care enough about her not to be the worst friends in the world, so why should she be worried if Lucy feels embarrassed? They can glare at her all they like – it doesn't bother her in the slightest and she can't believe that she was ever friends with girls like that.

It really, one hundred percent, absolutely and totally does not bother her. Not even a little bit.

The rest of the drama lesson passes without incident and Tally says goodbye to Aleksandra before heading to maths with a sense of relief. All she wants to do now is sit quietly and work on the problems that are written on the board. She likes maths. Everything is either right or wrong and there are patterns that make it easy to figure out what you need to do.

Except today, the problems written on the board are not like the ones that Mr Simpson usually gives the class.

"We're going to be working on our problem-solving skills," he tells them, handing out their exercise books. "Each of the questions on the board have several different steps for you to solve before you can work out the final answer. And the first step is identifying the actual question."

Tally stares at the board. Instead of numbers, it is covered with words, and the harder she looks, the more they seem to be leaping around and jumbling themselves up until nothing she reads makes any sense. This isn't how it's supposed to be. Maths is about numbers and logic, not rows and rows of sentences that she can't understand.

"You have four minutes to r   question and then work out your answer," Mr Simpson tells them. "I'll be choosing people at random to solve the problem, so don't even think about sitting back and relaxing because I could choose any single one of you!"

Tally swallows hard and tries to ignore the buzzing sound in her head. She hates it when teachers do this. They don't seem to understand that instead of helping people to focus on the task, it just makes everyone completely stressed. It's almost impossible to concentrate on work when you're utterly terrified that you're going to be picked on.

That's how it makes *her* feel, anyway. Maybe everyone else is fine with it, she doesn't really know.

"Three minutes left," bellows Mr Simpson, and Tally squeezes her hands into tight fists under the table. If he's going to count down every single minute like this then she's never going to be able to answer the question.

Your school is improving their environmental aware-ness because they've noticed that there is a lot of rubbish being thrown into landfill, which could be being recycled.

Tally has noticed this too and it's been bothering her for a while. In fact, only yesterday she saw one of the year nine boys throwing a Coke can into the general waste bin, even though the recycling bin was right next to it. When she pointed this out he just laughed and told her that she was welcome to get the can out and put it in the right bin if it mattered that much to her. She tried to tell him that it should matter to him too, because doesn't he watch the news? Hasn't he realized that it's up to *them* to save the planet before it's too late? Doesn't he lie awake at night worrying that the whole world is getting messed up and destroyed and hardly anyone grown-up seems to be doing anything about it?

But he just walked off with his mates and she was left to decide whether saving the world was a good enough reason to put her arm into the horrible bin and retrieve the can, which in all honesty was a very tricky decision to make. But she didn't really have a choice because a person can't really choose to *not* save the world, can they? And then it made the rest of the day a very *bad day* because even though she went straight to the bathrooms and scrubbed her hands as thoroughly as she could afterwards, she knew that the gross bin germs were still on her.

She returns her attention to the maths problem.

Everyone starts to recycle and by the end of the week there is a lot of rubbish to sort.

Sorting the rubbish is not a job that Tally would like to have to do. But someone has to do it and maybe she should volunteer to help out? She could wear rubber gloves and have a really long shower afterwards. Helping sort the recycling is the kind of thing that someone who cares about the future of the planet would do, and Tally cares, she really does. There are other things that she could do too. She's noticed that the lights are left on in all the classrooms at Kingswood Academy *all* the time, even when there's nobody in them. When she was in primary school she was a light monitor and it was her job to make sure that the lights were turned off if they weren't needed. It got her into trouble on one or two occasions, especially when she kept trying to turn off the staffroom lights at lunchtime – it might have been quite dark, but the teachers had more than enough light to eat their cheese sandwiches and drink their coffee, didn't they? Maybe she could ask Mrs Jarman about being a light monitor for the rest of this year?

"One minute left!" shouts Mr Simpson and Tally jumps in her seat. She's not sure what happened to two minutes but she's hardly got any time to work out this stupid maths problem now.

Two twelfths of the rubbish is books. One sixth of the rubbish is boxes. One third of the rubbish is bottles. Two sixths of the rubbish is cans. How much of the rubbish is paper products?

Why is the school throwing away books? That makes no sense. Tally blinks and looks at the board again, checking that her eyes aren't playing tricks on her. But it says quite clearly that two twelfths of the rubbish is books, which is utterly ridiculous because nobody should ever throw a book away, especially not in a school.

Although there was that one time Tally herself threw a book away. She's felt pretty guilty about it ever since, particularly as it was a library book. She knew that it wasn't an OK thing to do, but she couldn't help it. She was really enjoying the story to start with, and she even thought that the main character was a little bit like her. And then another girl came along and she was so horrible and mean that it was more than Tally could bear. It wouldn't have been so bad if the awful girl had ever learnt her lesson, but she just kept getting away with her terrible behaviour and it was all too much. Tally had thrown the book in the bin, slammed the lid down and instantly felt much better.

That was until Mum asked where her library book was and she had to pretend it had gone missing. She felt really bad about that, especially when Mum had to pay the library for the cost of a replacement book. Even secretly putting her pocket money into Mum's purse to pay her back didn't make the nasty, swirling guilty feeling go away.

"Your time is up!" shouts Mr Simpson. "Let's see who is going to solve the first problem." His eyes dart around the room and Tally looks down at the desk, desperate not to be chosen.

"Up you get, Ameet! You are lucky contestant number one!" Mr Simpson points at Ameet, assuming the role of a quizmaster. "How much of the rubbish is paper products?"

Ameet pushes his chair back and stands up.

"It's easy, isn't it? Books are paper so the answer is two twelfths."

Mr Simpson makes a buzzer noise. "Uh-uh. You are eliminated from the game. Time for lucky contestant number two. Drumroll, please."

Everyone starts banging their hands on the desks and it takes every bit of strength that Tally has not to slam her hands over her ears.

"Stand up, Tally! Can you do better than our previous answer? How much of the rubbish is paper products?"

Tally forces herself to raise her head and look at the teacher. She can sense the rest of the class staring at her and even if she *had* got as far as working out the answer, the pressure building in her head right now would be enough to chase it out of her mind.

Slowly, and with shaking legs, she gets up.

"The clock is ticking, Tally!" Mr Simpson informs her. "I'm afraid that I'm going to need your answer immediately."

The kid sitting next to her starts making a tick-tocking sound and Tally forgets the question. All she can think about is the world burning because nobody at this school will even recycle a Coke can, while Mr Simpson stands at the front of the class making ridiculous jokes that aren't even funny. She wants to tell him that it's a stupid question so it's probably got a stupid answer, but she doesn't dare be that rude to a teacher and besides, she doesn't think any words would come out even if she did open her mouth. So instead, she stands silently, hoping that he'll understand and pick on someone else.

"Hurry up! We're all waiting for your answer!"

He doesn't understand. She doesn't know why she thought he might. Mr Simpson doesn't know her, not really, which is kind of not his fault. Tally has worked really hard to make him think that she's just the same as everyone else, plus she's been doing really well in his class up until now, when the questions have been *proper* maths questions.

"I thought you'd have got this one," Mr Simpson says, looking disappointed. "You can sit down, but start paying attention, please. Don't waste valuable lesson time daydreaming."

He turns and points at one of the kids in the back row, gesturing for them to stand up and solve the problem.

"How about you, Jamie? Are you going to put us all out of our misery and answer the question correctly?"

Jamie shrugs. "Well, the books and the boxes are both made out of paper," he starts. "And we need to make all the denominators the same before we can compare the fractions – but that's easy because they can all be converted into sixths."

"That's wrong," mutters Tally quietly, shaking her head. "Books aren't rubbish."

Jamie stops talking and everyone, including Mr Simpson, looks at her. She obviously wasn't quite as quiet as she thought she was.

"What was that?" asks Mr Simpson, tilting his head to one side. "What did you say about the books?"

"They aren't rubbish," Tally whispers. "So they shouldn't be thrown away."

Mr Simpson frowns. "This is a maths lesson," he tells her. "Whether the books should or should not be thrown away isn't the point. You need to read the question carefully and give an answer that is based on the numbers."

He looks around at the whole class. "It's *all* about the numbers, people – never forget that. Now, Jamie – please tell us what we do to the numerator once we've turned twelfths into sixths."

Tally sinks into her chair, biting her lip in an attempt not to cry. Mr Simpson doesn't have a clue. If this lesson had been about the numbers then she could have answered the question easily. It's *him* that has made everything confusing by using words that don't make any sense. And it just isn't fair for him to accuse her of wasting her time daydreaming when it would be a whole lot easier to pay attention if people stopped making everything quite so difficult.

CHAPTER 5

It's Sunday – Tally's worst day of the week. Everybody else
that she knows hates Monday the most but Tally thinks
that Sunday is definitely the hardest day. She's given it a
lot of thought and decided that the reason she dislikes
Sunday so much is because it's a fake. It pretends to be all
fantastic and *weekendy*, but the fact is that on Sunday, you
can't ever forget that the week is looming ahead and the
anticipation of having to go to school is lurking in every
second. At least Monday is honest. It knows it's rubbish
and it doesn't pretend to be anything else.

This particular Sunday is trickier than most and it isn't
about to get any better. What Tally really needs is a chill-
out and a rest after the last few days, but Dad has ruined
any chance of that, which seems completely unfair when
the end of last week was so difficult.

When Tally got home from school on Thursday, after the drama lesson with Lucy and then the maths lesson with Mr Simpson, Mum made the mistake of asking if she had any homework to do. Tally *did* have homework and she *had* intended on doing it after she'd had a snack and played with Rupert. But Mum spoilt her plan by asking her about it, and by the time she'd stopped feeling upset, she was too tired to do anything except go to bed.

It was a shame that two of the coffee mugs got broken but Mum shouldn't have made that sighing noise when Tally told her that she was ruining her life. That wasn't helpful. She didn't mean to break the mugs. That's the hardest thing about meltdowns – when you can't control your brain or body then things can happen that you didn't plan on doing or saying.

And now all she wants to do is keep making her video but Dad won't leave her alone.

"What do you think about this top?" he asks, holding up a blue-and-white stripy sweatshirt. "It could be good for the evenings when it gets a bit cooler, and you've always loved wearing it."

"Whatever." Tally looks back at her screen. She knows that if Dad stops distracting her then she can make her best TikTok ever, and that is far more important to her right now than a sweatshirt. He's wrong anyway; she totally hates that top now. It gives her a headache whenever she looks at it and if Dad packs it in her bag then she's never going to wear it, no matter how cold it might be. Mum would know that but Mum isn't here. She's out with Nell and so Tally has to put up with Dad and his uneducated opinion on her favourite clothes.

"We need to pack your swimming things," he continues. "Can you go and choose a towel from the airing cupboard, please?"

Tally ignores him and swivels round on her bed so that her back is towards him. Maybe he'll get the message and go away.

"Tally." Dad's voice is gentle but Tally can hear that he's serious. "We agreed that we'd pack your bag today, remember? You promised us that you'd help if Mum took you shopping yesterday."

She presses "record" and starts to make her video. And then Dad stands up and Tally sees him on her phone screen, looking over her shoulder.

"You've ruined my TikTok!" Her words fire out of her mouth like bullets, zooming around the room until they find Dad. "Now I'm going to have to start all over again which means that I haven't got time to pack my stupid bag so you'll have to do it yourself."

She throws her phone on the bed and scowls. If she's honest, she'd rather watch Peppa Pig than go on TikTok, but the fear of being caught watching a baby programme means she can't let herself relax in the way that she wants to. Dad always tells her that nobody would ever know, but Dad doesn't understand – the kids at school have a way of finding that kind of stuff out. She didn't think anyone would ever know about her tiger mask and look what happened there.

"Actually, don't bother packing anything," she tells him now. "I'm not going on the school trip anyway."

Dad gets up from the floor and walks across to the bed where Tally is sitting.

"We've been through this, sweetheart," he says, perching on the mattress beside her. "You're going to love it when you get there."

Tally throws herself back on to her duvet and stares up at the ceiling.

"How dare you tell me that I'm going to love it?" Her voice is low and filled with fury. "You aren't me, are you? I might have a terrible time. I might fall in the lake and drown. I might tumble off a cliff and die. I might get kidnapped and you'll never see me again." She twists her head to look at Dad. "Do you even know me? Do you have any idea about how scary it is being me? Have you actually given *any thought at all* to my safety?"

Dad nods solemnly. "I have. So has Mum. We've spent a long time thinking about whether it's safe for you to go and we've come to one, very important, conclusion."

"And what's that?" Tally closes her eyes, trying to block out the scary images that are flickering across her brain like a film reel.

"We've decided that it's far more dangerous for you *not* to go on this trip," Dad says. "We could keep you at home and never let you go anywhere, but that wouldn't be right, Tally. The best way for you to be safe is for you to have new experiences and figure out new ways of dealing with things."

Tally opens her eyes and stares at Dad.

"That's silly. Staying at home isn't dangerous. If I stay here then I'll be perfectly safe."

Dad nods. "For now. But one day you're going to be out in the big, wide world."

"You're making it sound like the story of the Three Little Pigs," snorts Tally, sitting up and swinging her legs over the side of the bed. "Are you going to throw me out of the house and send me off to make my living?"

Dad laughs. "Not quite. But we won't always be there to help you and I'd like to think that any daughter of mine would know to build a house out of bricks, not straw!"

"I bet Nell would totally choose straw," says Tally, choosing to ignore the very daft comment about Mum and Dad not always being there to help her because they're her parents. Of course they'll always be there.

Dad stands up and walks across to where Tally's bag is lying on the floor. "I don't think that's true. Nell went on the GoCamp trip when she was in year seven and she came back with a ton of useful skills. Plus, she had a great time."

Tally frowns. Just because Nell had a good time does not mean that it's going to be the same for her.

"Don't forget that Mrs Jarman is going to be there with you," says Dad, staring at the massive pile of clothes in front of him. "She's said that you can go to her any time if you feel worried or you have a problem. Mum says that she's very nice."

"She is," agrees Tally, tapping her hands on her knees. Mrs Jarman was the person who told her that she shouldn't waste any more time trying to be like other people and that it's OK to just be *her*. She *sees* Tally and she knows who she really is. Having just one teacher at school who understands her has made year seven much more bearable and, even though most lessons are still really tough, being able to be truly herself in drama class sometimes feels like the only thing keeping her going when everything else is so hard.

"So my thinking is – you should go on the trip and see how you feel," Dad continues. "Because otherwise you're letting your worries decide what you do. You are fierce and wonderful and determined and you are capable of doing anything, even the things that might frighten you. You just need to be in charge of the choosing." Tally thinks about this for a moment. Lots of things frighten her and she isn't sure if Dad is right when he says that she can do anything, because has he even *seen* her trying to skip with a rope? But she doesn't want to let her worries choose what she does or doesn't get to do, he's definitely right about that. Her worries get in the way too much as it is. Maybe she can squash them down like one of her squishy toys and make her own mind up for once.

"Fine. I'll give it a go. But what about Rupert?" It's the same question that she has asked approximately one hundred times since the topic of the trip was first raised. "Who is going to look after him?"

Dad sighs. It's a very small sigh but Tally hears it, all the same.

"I'm going to walk him every day," he tells her, also for the hundredth time. "And Mum is going to make sure that he's eaten his food."

Tally shakes her head. "That's not what I mean," she says. "I mean, who is going to look after him? Who is going to check that he isn't feeling stressed while I'm away? Who is going to talk to him and tell him about what's happening each day? You know, the important stuff?"

Dad smiles. "I absolutely promise that we will all make sure Rupert isn't pining away without you. Me, Mum and Nell – we'll all take care of him. Which socks do you want to take?"

"Dogs can have terrible separation anxiety," Tally tells him, sitting down on the floor and picking up a pair of socks. They're the special ones without a seam so she puts them into her bag and then starts sifting through a pile of T-shirts, looking for any that are purple, her favourite colour. "You need to be alert, OK? He might start whining or stop eating and sleeping. You might need to let him sleep with something that reminds him of me."

Dad nods. "Understood. Do you want to take the blue pyjamas or the purple ones?"

Tally points to the purple pyjamas and finds another pair of socks to put in the bag. "You could always let him sleep in my room, if he gets really sad."

"I'll keep that suggestion in mind," Dad tells her. "But I think Rupert is going to be fine. And just think how happy he's going to be to see you when you get home."

Tally thinks that probably, Rupert would be even happier if she didn't go away in the first place, but she can tell that Dad has had enough of talking and just wants to get her bag packed, so she decides to be kind and keep her opinion to herself.

Date: Sunday 14th June.

Situation: Packing for camp.

Anxiety rating: 8. There are a million reasons why I don't want to go to camp and quite honestly, it's a miracle that I haven't had a stress breakdown today. The only reason that I haven't is because I've spent most of the day with Rupert and he always helps to keep me calm.

Dear Diary,

The day is finally almost here. Tomorrow I go on the school residential trip, and my head is so full of worries that I feel like I'm going to explode. I've had my Worry Window time and talked to Mum about everything that's on my mind and honestly, I'm done with thinking about it.

So let's talk about my favourite thing to talk about. You've guessed it – Rupert! I've decided that when I'm old enough to make all my own decisions I will have a house full of free-ranging pets.

In my opinion animals are the best sort of best friends and here's why:

- They feel so good to touch and are always up for a cuddle.

- Even when it's silent, it's never awkward.

- You can learn how to make friends by watching them.

- They don't judge you, ever.

- You don't have to mask with them.

- There is actual research done that says that autistic kids with dogs have fewer meltdowns than those without. This is because when a kid is stressed, they can turn to the dog for comfort and it can help them calm down.

- They never, ever make you stressed or upset like humans do.

- The worst they might do is annoy you a tiny bit, and when you tell them off for it, they just get over it really quickly and you can both move on. Like when Rupert nicked my giant cookie the other day. I had left half of it for a treat after doing my dreaded homework. I went to finish it and it had disappeared. Maybe it's just me but the feeling of not having finished half a cookie is just the worst! Rupert got a lot of insults thrown at him by me that day, I can tell you! Which leads me to my last point...

- Animals don't get mortally offended like humans do when someone like me occasionally gets stressed and says unkind things to them. They don't care. Maybe they just know that it's only the anger from anxiety talking, and if you just ignore it or are really friendly it will go away soon. Rupert just wags his tail and nuzzles me and I'm over it straight away and can be nice again. I wish humans could do this more, but they get all wounded and outraged and then start using that high-pitched angry voice that makes me panic and be even more rude and defiant. It's a vicious circle. I'm always trying to tell my parents this. I don't MEAN the things I say. I told my dad once to try and imagine he has just pressed a button on a computerized random insult generator when I'm being horrible to him. The things I say might be awful, terrible things, like I wish he would die a horrible death, but of course I don't mean them. They come out of nowhere sometimes and even shock me. And the more he gets upset, the more awful I feel once I've calmed down, and the more I start to worry that I'm giving them a terrible life and then that's just another thing to add to my list of worries. My family are getting better at understanding this now, and I know they work hard to try not to take my outbursts personally. But Rupert is even better at it. When I called him a greedy, disgusting dog for nicking my biscuit he just came up and put his paws on my lap and licked my ear and I was instantly destressed and able to be nice again. I'm not saying I want my family to lick my ears. Nell did that once in a restaurant when we were much younger. She had ice cubes in her mouth and wanted to surprise me by showing me how cold her tongue was. It did not end well for her – or the chair she was sitting on.

Anyway, back to animals. Dogs are especially good pets for autistic kids as they show how they are feeling through the way they behave, unlike cats, where you really have to work hard to suss out what they are thinking. And dogs are great for practising how to read body language, which is something some autistic people can struggle with. Some can't work out what neurotypical people mean with their little gestures and facial expressions. Others, like me, are hypersensitive to body language, so I notice even just a small sigh and it can go a longer way than you might think. It really triggers me if I can feel somebody is annoyed with me, and that stress comes out as anger. I don't get at the time that it's just a temporary feeling for them. In my mind it's catastrophic. But dogs do none of this sighing and rolling of their eyes and thinking they are hiding their annoyance when in fact they are letting it seep out in other ways that I can spot just as easily. Dogs never try to hide how they are feeling. You always know where you are with a dog, and that's what I love about them most.

But really, any pet can make a difference. I used to have a hamster called Fudge and she would always sit and cuddle up on my lap, even though people say you can't usually train hamsters to do that.

Even something such as a fish can help relax the brain and can help with stress as looking at them swimming around is so calming. They aren't so good for giving you a cuddle at the end of a bad day, though.

CHAPTER 6

"I'm not going."

Mum doesn't answer. She just keeps on doing up the zip on Tally's bag, as if she hasn't even heard her.

"I said, I am not going on this stupid trip and you can't make me!" Tally raises her voice and sticks her chin in the air. They've said all along that it's her decision to make, so she's making it and that's final.

"I'm sure that everyone in year seven is probably feeling a bit worried this morning," Mum says, sticking her head round the front door and looking at Tally. "It's completely normal to have last-minute nerves."

Tally snorts but doesn't bother to reply. She can't think of a single person at her school who would describe her as "normal", and she also can't begin to imagine any of the rest of them feeling anxious about the camping trip. Why would they, when it's all so easy for them?

"Just remember what we talked about last night." Mum picks up the bag and takes it over to the drive, forcing Tally to step outside if she wants to continue having this conversation. "You've got lots of strategies to help you if things feel a bit tricky. We've packed your journal so you can get all your thoughts out, and Mrs Jarman will always be close by if you need a friendly face to chat to. It's only for five days, Tally – you'll be home on Friday with a bag full of dirty clothes and a whole lot of stories to tell!"

Tally shudders. She doesn't want her clothes to get dirty and she's fairly sure that any stories she has will be firmly placed in the horror section.

"You can't make me—" she starts and then a car pulls up and suddenly Aleksandra is there, waving excitedly out of the window.

"I thought it would be nice for us all to go together," Mum says, giving Tally a quick look. "Aleksandra's mum kindly offered to give us a lift."

Tally opens her mouth to start telling Mum exactly what she thinks of her ambushing the situation like this, but then she closes it again. Aleksandra and her mum are right there and she hates the idea of anyone else knowing how upset she can get with Mum and Dad. She knows she shouldn't behave the way that she sometimes does, but it's not as if she chooses it. The meltdowns happen when she's at her most worried and scared, but she works super-hard not to let people see how stressed she can get. She can delay a meltdown when she's around others, but it has to come out sooner or later. They can't stay buried inside her for long – it's impossible to think about anything else when she can feel the fear and fury churning in her head.

She's wondered before why the meltdowns always come at home and never at school and the only answer she's got is that, no matter how angry she gets or how frightened the world makes her, Mum and Dad will always love her just the same. It used to worry her a lot when she was younger – that one day she'd go too far and maybe they'd decide that they didn't want her any more and run away. But she's had some pretty bad times and they're still here.

The same definitely cannot be said for her so-called friends.

"Tally!" yells Aleksandra, winding down the window. "Let's go! We don't want to miss the coach!"

Tally would like nothing more than to miss the coach. She imagines it pulling off down the road, a big swirl of dust behind it and when the dust finally clears, the coach and the rest of year seven will have magically disappeared.

"I don't want to go," she whispers to Mum, turning away from the car. "Please don't make me."

Mum takes a few steps forward and pulls her in for a big hug. "It's going to be OK," she murmurs against Tally's head. Her voice sounds a bit sniffly and Tally wonders if Mum is about to start crying. She pulls away quickly – she's got enough to worry about without adding Mum humiliating her to the list.

"I know what you're doing," Tally tells her quietly. She can see that Aleksandra's mum getting out of the car and she doesn't want her to hear. "You planned for them to come here so that I *have* to go. But I don't have to like it and I don't have to forgive you for tricking me."

"It's not a trick," Mum says. "Sometimes it's easier to do things with a friend, that's all."

"Whatever." Tally glares at Mum. "But if the coach crashes on the way to the camp or I get food poisoning and die then just remember that it will all be your fault. Just like it'll be your fault when I have a terrible time and spend the whole week feeling sad."

"Tally—" starts Mum, but Tally doesn't let her continue.

"I have to say goodbye to Rupert," she tells her. "Seeing

as he's the only member of this family who actually cares about me."

Mum gives her head a quick shake.

"We all care about you, Tally. Dad left you that lovely note on the breakfast table this morning and Nell made a point of coming to say goodbye to you before she went to school." She pauses and takes a big breath. "I am really, truly sorry if I've made you feel pressured into going on the trip. It's your trip and it's your choice. If you really feel that you can't go then that's OK with me. You know what you can and can't do – I know that you can choose for yourself."

Tally stares at Mum suspiciously, certain that this is another trick.

"Do you mean it?" she asks. "Are you really saying that I don't have to go?"

Mum nods and gives Tally a smile. "Yes."

"But what about Aleksandra and her mum?"

Mum reaches out and takes hold of Tally's hand. "I'll tell them to go on without us," she says. "It's not a big deal."

Tally bites her lip. "I don't know what to choose," she whispers. "It's too hard."

Mum leads her up the path and towards the front door

where they can't be overheard.

"Trust yourself," she tells her. "You have a wonderful and very brilliant brain in that head of yours and it knows what you want to do. You just have to listen to what it's telling you."

Tally squeezes her eyes shut and listens but the only thing she can hear is the engine running on Aleksandra's mum's car and a particularly noisy pigeon, cooing in the tree by the garden gate.

"Is your brain telling you that it's a definite *no* to going to GoCamp?" asks Mum, quietly. "Or is it saying that it thinks it might be fun to go but there are a lot of worries to think about?"

Tally opens her eyes. "There *are* a lot of worries," she agrees.

"Are they worries that you can do something about?" Mum's voice is calm and relaxed, like she could spend all day standing on the front step chatting. Tally wonders if calmness is contagious because the longer she stands here with Mum, the less her heart is pounding.

"Well, I'm worried about being on my own," she confesses.

"Tally! Come on! We're going to have an amazing time!" calls Aleksandra, right on cue.

"I don't think that you're going to be alone," says Mum, giving Aleksandra a wave.

Tally opens her mouth to tell her that this is another big worry – not having any time on her own to chill out and relax – but then she closes it again. It's time to make a choice and she knows what that choice has to be. If she goes on the trip then there are one hundred things that *could* go wrong, but if she doesn't go then she'll *definitely* miss out on everything.

Tally blinks rapidly and then pulls her hand out of Mum's. She can do this, but she has to say goodbye to Rupert first.

In the kitchen, Rupert is lying on his bed. He wags his tail as she approaches and she sinks down on to her knees next him. He flops his head on to her lap and she starts to stroke him, gazing down into his big, chocolate eyes.

"It's going to be OK," she tells him. "You can do this."

She drops her head on top of his and lets a few tears mingle with his fur. She can't cry in front of anyone else, but Rupert doesn't judge her. She can be herself when she's with him. He nudges her face with his nose and she knows that he understands.

"I love you, boy," she whispers. "I really, really do love you. Be brave and I'll be home soon." She hesitates and then says it anyway. "I promise."

She never promises anything to anyone because it's a stupid thing to do. Tally doesn't know what might happen in the future and neither does anyone else. If you make promises then you're just setting yourself up to be a liar.

Standing up, and hoping that she isn't about break his trust, she grits her teeth and walks out of the kitchen.

Aleksandra chatters about the trip the entire way to school. Tally tries to ignore her but her excitement is quite infectious, and by the time they reach the car park, both girls are craning out of the window to see if they can spot the coaches.

"Excellent!" declares Aleksandra. "There's loads of people here but the coaches haven't arrived yet. We're not too late!" She turns to Tally. "We do *not* want to have to sit at the front with the kids who get travel sick!"

Tally nods in agreement. She absolutely doesn't want to be near anybody who has the remotest chance of being sick. The very idea makes her feel ill.

"Have a wonderful time, girls!" says Aleksandra's mum, once they've found a parking space and are out of the car. "It's going to be a marvellous adventure!"

"We will!" Aleksandra tells her, giving her a big hug. "Thanks, Mum! I'm so glad that I could go on this trip."

Her mum smiles, a huge smile that spreads from her mouth to her eyes.

"I'm glad too," she says to her and then she looks across at Tally's mum. "It was touch and go for a bit there trying to find the money, but we got there in the end!"

Tally's mum nods understandingly. "They cost us a fortune, these kids!"

"Shall we leave them to it, then?" asks Aleksandra's mum, gesturing at the car. "Unless you want to stay and wave them off on the coach?"

"Mum!" howls Aleksandra, pulling a face. "Don't you dare! How embarrassing would that be?"

Tally's mum turns to face her. "Would you like me to stay?" she asks quietly. "You can choose."

Tally has been thinking about this moment for the last few weeks. She has pictured the coach pulling away from school and Mum waving to her from the pavement, just like every time she's ever been on a school trip for the day. She likes knowing that Mum is there when she goes and will be right there, waiting for her to come back. She hadn't for one single second imagined that Mum might just leave her in the car park.

"No way," she says, pulling the same face that Aleksandra pulled. "How embarrassing would that be?"

"Are you sure?" Mum's face looks doubtful. "It's fine for me to stay for a few minutes."

"Don't you dare!" Tally almost shouts the words. It feels very, very wrong, but she can't start the trip looking different to everyone else, and if nobody else's parents are waving the coach off then her mum has got to go.

"Have a great time," Mum says, opening her arms. "Enjoy every moment, my lovely girl. I love you so much and you'll be in my mind all the time while you're away."

"Come on!" Aleksandra grabs her bag with one hand and Tally's arm with the other. Tally gives Mum a last, desperate glance and then she's speeding across to where hordes of year seven kids are piling onto one of the two coaches that have pulled up outside school.

"Just leave your bags here, girls," says Mr Kennedy, ticking their names off a list. "We'll make sure that they're all loaded on to the coach. Get on and find yourselves a seat."

Aleksandra pulls Tally up the steps and Tally is quite glad now that Mum arranged for them to arrive together. The idea of having to do all of this on her own is utterly terrifying. They push their way up the aisle, stepping over bags and stretched-out legs until Aleksandra stops and gently pushes Tally towards a seat.

"Amazing! We're almost at the back!" she says. "You can go by the window if you like."

Tally squeezes into the space and sinks down on to the seat, gazing out of the window to see if she can spot Mum. She didn't really mean it when she told her to go and she knows that Mum will know that. She'll be doing that thing where she waits somewhere out of the way, where only Tally can see her. And they'll do their special wave and it won't matter that she didn't have a goodbye hug and then all week, she'll be able to remember Mum waving her off and know that she's waiting right here for her to return.

But Mum isn't there, and as Tally stares, she sees the back of Aleksandra's Mum's car disappearing round a corner. Her heart starts to race and she clenches her fists as tightly as she can.

Mum left her.

How could she?

"Do you want a caramel?" asks Aleksandra, shoving a paper bag in front of Tally. "I've got loads."

Tally shakes her head and says nothing. She continues to say nothing as the coach fills up with kids and Aleksandra chatters about what the first activity might be when they arrive at GoCamp. She can't talk. She can't think about anything else but the churning sensation in her stomach and the murmuring voice in her head, telling her that Mum was glad to leave her and that it's a relief for her entire family to have five whole days without her.

That's why they wanted you to go, hisses the voice. *They wanted to have a break from you.*

"OK, everybody settle down, please." Mr Kennedy gets on to the bus and claps his hands loudly. "Now, just a few things to say before we can get on our way. The first is that there is to be no eating and drinking on the coach."

A loud booing noise fills the air and Mr Kennedy raises his hand.

"It's a two-hour journey and I'm fairly sure that you can all cope for that long without sustenance. Secondly, and the driver has asked me to say this, do NOT put your feet on the seats. Apparently the last time we booked these coaches, they were left in such a state that they required a deep clean afterwards. You wouldn't put your feet on the furniture at home, would you?"

"I would!" yells Luke. "My mum doesn't care!"

"Yes, well – don't do it here, please," snaps Mr Kennedy. "And thirdly, Mrs Jarman is unable to attend, so Miss Perkins has very kindly agreed to step in at the last minute. If you were in Mrs Jarman's group before then you'll be in her group now."

He glances at his watch. "I think that's everything. I will be travelling on the other coach, so I'm leaving Miss Perkins in charge and any reports of poor behaviour will be dealt with on our arrival."

He gives them all one last glare and then stomps off the coach. The engine rumbles to life and the coach pulls off. Everyone gives a massive cheer and then breaks out into a rousing rendition of "One Hundred Green Bottles".

Everyone except Tally. She just stares out of the window, watching as familiar landmarks slide past and then vanish. She keeps looking until they're out of town and on to the main road and the scenery stops feeling like home, and then she slumps into her seat and tries to pretend that she's sitting on top of the garden shed with Rupert waiting for her down below.

"Shame about Mrs Jarman, isn't it?" says Aleksandra, who has given up on trying to get Tally to talk and is now deep in conversation with Mina, who is sitting across the aisle. "I don't like Miss Perkins. She shouts all the time and she gave me a detention last term because I forgot my PE kit."

Tally does not want to hear this. She's been trying to pretend that what Mr Kennedy said about Mrs Jarman isn't true, because if it is, and she isn't coming on the trip, then everything is not just wrong; it's catastrophic. Mrs Jarman was the only reason she ever agreed to this whole thing.

Someone starts throwing sweets in the air and they rain down like giant hailstones. The noise in the coach swells like waves in a storm and Tally closes her eyes, wishing that they'd all just disappear.

"Why are you talking to *her*, anyway?" she mutters to Aleksandra, waving in the direction of Mina. "You're sitting next to *me*. You should only be talking to me."

Aleksandra makes a small sound. It is the tiniest of tiny sighs, but Tally can't blame her. She isn't being any fun to be with, she knows that. Aleksandra has been looking forward to this trip and now Tally is spoiling it, just like she always does.

This is exactly the time that she needs to find Mrs Jarman and ask for a quiet time out. But she isn't here.

Tally is one hundred percent on her own.

CHAPTER 7

The journey seems to take forever.

Outside the window, the world looks different now. There are hardly any buildings and all Tally can see is field after field. The coach turns off the main road and starts winding its way down a steep hill, twisting and turning round the sharp bends. Tally's tummy flips over and she clenches her fists hard. She can't get sick. Not now.

"Are you OK?" asks Aleksandra, turning to look at her. "Your face has gone a bit pale."

Tally wants to tell her that actually, no – she isn't OK. Not even a tiny bit. She's stuck on this coach and the stuffy air that is probably filled with everyone else's germs is making her throat feel tight, like she can't really breathe. And she can't even distract herself by playing on her phone because Mr Kennedy has gone on and on about the trip being "technology-free" and nobody has been allowed to bring any devices with them. She isn't sure how she's supposed to cope without her phone.

Tally wants to tell Aleksandra that she needs someone to help her. But if she opens her mouth then she might throw up, and that cannot be allowed to happen. So instead she presses her lips together and looks back out of the window, trying to tell herself that just because Aleksandra sighs and goes back to talking to Mina, it doesn't mean that she isn't a good friend. Mum is always telling her that people aren't mind readers but surely if Aleksandra cared about her at all then she'd know how to make Tally feel better?

The coach makes one more turn and suddenly, without any warning, the view changes.

"I can see the sea!" Tally yells, her churning stomach forgotten. "Look! Over there!"

There is something about the sea that always makes Tally feel good. No, not good. It makes her feel *calm*, like everything in the world is going to work out OK. She likes the hugeness, and when she stands in front of the waves, she feels part of something bigger – like maybe things aren't as complicated as people are always making them out to be. The sea has rules. The tide ebbs and flows and the waves build up and then break.

Floating in the sea is Tally's favourite thing to do in the entire world. It's like a ready-made sensory extravaganza. The smell of the salt and the sounds of the waves. The sunlight bouncing off the surface of the water and the feeling of being suspended, like she's flying. The only thing better than actually being in the sea is sitting on the beach, all cuddled up in her special, heavy blanket and watching the waves as the sun starts to set.

"I can see the sea!" she calls again. Maybe this trip isn't going to be so bad after all.

The coach goes silent for a second and she smiles, waiting for everyone to react.

"Ooh, the *sea*." The voice of the person who is sitting behind her does not sound particularly excited. In fact, it sounds distinctly sarcastic which Tally does not like one bit. It's impossible to understand what people mean when their words are saying one thing but their tone is saying something quite different. You have to choose which one to listen to and it makes everything one hundred times more difficult.

"Is she for real?" mutters someone else. "Hasn't she seen the sea before?"

"I hope you packed your bucket and spade!" yells

Ameet from the back row and everyone starts laughing.

"Just ignore them," murmurs Aleksandra. "They'll get bored in a minute." She puts her hand on Tally's arm and gives her a sympathetic smile. "I think we're nearly there now, anyway."

The coach turns inland and the sea disappears from view. Tally feels her stomach start to swirl again, and for a brief moment she thinks that being sick is a very real possibility. But then Aleksandra's hand tightens on her arm, reminding her that she isn't alone, and the horrible sensation eases slightly. Aleksandra is here and she's a good friend. Tally knows that sometimes she can get jealous. Mum has spoken to her about it before and Tally has been working really hard not to mind when Aleksandra talks to other people. Mum called it her "green-eyed monster", which Tally thought was a very silly way to describe it. The feeling she gets when she thinks that Aleksandra would rather be hanging out with someone else isn't *green* in the slightest.

It's red.

Hot, molten-lava red.

The kind of red that you see if you shut your eyes tight and squeeze them together.

The kind of red that rages and burns, long after everyone else has forgotten about it.

Tally knows that her "red-eyed monster" has a very long memory.

The coach pulls through some gates and heads down a long drive. Up ahead, Tally can see a group of buildings and the other half of the year group clambering off the second coach.

"They're going to get all the best cabins!" yells a girl at the front and suddenly there's a mass panic as everyone gets up and surges down the aisle, despite Miss Perkins shouting and telling everyone to sit down and wait their turn.

Aleksandra waits until everyone else has left the coach and then stands up.

"Come on!" Aleksandra's eyes are sparkling as she peers out of the window. "We're going to have the best time, Tally!"

Tally nods, feeling a surge of excitement. They're here. She's got her friend and everything is going to be absolutely fine.

She can do this.

Outside, everyone is huddled in little groups. Mr Kennedy and Miss Perkins help the drivers to pull the luggage out of the hold and heap it up into a huge pile.

Tally looks anxiously at where she can see her bright purple bag getting squashed by someone else's suitcase. Mum packed energy bars and some of her favourite biscuits, just in case she doesn't like the food here. They'll be smashed into crumbs if Miss Perkins loads anything else on top.

"Quieten down!" yells Mr Kennedy once all the bags are off and the coaches have pulled away. "The first thing that we're going to do is send you off in groups to settle into your new home for the week. When you hear your name, collect your bag and follow the signs on the trees to find your designated accommodation. Tents are to the right in the South Field and cabins are to the left in the North Field."

"I'm so glad that we both chose to be in a cabin," Tally says, smiling at Aleksandra. "I hate camping. All those spiders!"

Her friend turns to look at her.

"A cabin? But I didn't—" she starts.

"The following people are in the South Field," shouts Miss Perkins, drowning her out. "In Tent One, we have Luke and Ameet."

"Is that it?" asks Luke, barging past Tally and making his way to where the teachers are standing. "We've got a tent all to ourselves?"

"Sweet!" adds Ameet. "Nobody to annoy us!"

Mr Kennedy shakes his head. "It's just you two from *our* school," he corrects. "You'll meet your new tent-mates when you get there, as we already explained in the briefing session." He turns to face Miss Perkins. "I believe they've already arrived?"

She nods. "Apparently they got here an hour ago. They're just waiting for us to get sorted and then we can all have lunch."

"We'd better get a move on then." Mr Kennedy claps his hands. "Now, I'm sure that I don't need to remind you all that you are representing Kingswood Academy and your behaviour needs to be exemplary throughout our time here. If there are any issues then I won't hesitate to phone your parents and ask them to remove you from the site. Is that understood?"

There is a general muttering sound and Mr Kennedy scowls.

"I said, IS THAT UNDERSTOOD?" he bellows and Tally jumps, her hands flying to her ears before she can stop them.

"Yes, sir!" chants the majority of year seven.

"Excellent," he replies. "And, as we all know the importance of first impressions, you need to head straight to your accommodation so that we aren't making your new friends wait too much longer for their lunch."

Luke rolls his eyes at Ameet.

"They're from Redhill High," he smirks. "I'm pretty sure we won't be finding any new friends from there!"

"Just get on with it," barks Miss Perkins, reading from the clipboard in her hands. "Now, in Tent Two we have Carla, Rosie and Yvette."

Tally watches as the three girls collect their bags and set off, laughing excitedly. The sunlight is pouring through the trees, making puddles of warmth on the path, and the whole place looks friendly and inviting.

"Layla, Lucy, Ayesha and Tally – you're in Cabin One," calls Mr Kennedy. "Grab your bags, girls and head over to the North Field."

Three of the girls move towards the pile of bags. The fourth stays very still, her feet firmly planted on the ground.

This is all going very, very wrong.

"And in Tent Three, we have Mina and Aleksandra," says Miss Perkins.

Just in front of them, Mina squeals and then spins to look at Aleksandra.

"We're together!" she says. "I was hoping we would be. I've hardly seen you this term, Alek!"

Tally looks down at the ground, pressing her arms to her sides as hard as she can. Whenever she gets worried or scared, her arms need to flap, but she can't let that happen. Not here. Not in front of everyone.

"Tally, I didn't know you'd chosen a cabin," Aleksandra tells her, as Mina grabs her hand. "I'm sure we can ask for you to be put in our tent."

Tally ignores her. She wrote *one* name on her piece of paper, when she was choosing who she wanted to be with. *One name*. And Mrs Jarman promised her and Mum that she'd be with Aleksandra, no matter what.

But Aleksandra had to write a name too. And now Tally is sure that the name her so-called best friend wrote down did not begin with a "T".

"Come on!" Mina starts pulling Aleksandra in the direction of the bags. "I want to find our tent and meet our new tent-mates!"

"Ask if you can swap!" calls Aleksandra as she moves off. "Ask now, Tally!"

Kids are starting to move as their names are called but Tally stands motionless, as if she's rooted to the spot. Eventually, everyone has collected their luggage and the only thing left is one bright purple bag.

The teachers turn away and for a brief moment, Tally thinks that she might be left all alone. The terror makes her feet start moving and she's at their side in seconds, darting in front of them to get their attention.

"Tally!" says Mr Kennedy, as if he's surprised to even see her on the trip. "You're supposed to be finding your way to your accommodation with everyone else." He glances behind her and frowns. "Is that your bag?"

"I want to swap with someone." The words rip out of her mouth before she can take them back. She doesn't want to sleep in a tent. It will be cold and uncomfortable and it'll smell strange and not even a little bit like home. But she wants to be without Aleksandra even less.

Miss Perkins wrinkles her forehead and consults the clipboard.

"You're in Cabin One," she says, as if that answers the problem. "If you head down this path and turn left, it should be at the end."

"No." Tally's voice is so quiet that she can't be entirely sure that she's even spoken. "I don't want to be in Cabin One. I want to be with my friend."

Miss Perkins gives Mr Kennedy *the look*. It's amazing how much a person can say without using any words and what Miss Perkins is saying right now isn't actually very nice.

"And you *are* with your friends," she tells Tally, using the kind of voice that people use when they're talking to a baby. "You're with Layla, Lucy and Ayesha and you're always hanging around with them at school, aren't you!"

Not any more, thinks Tally. *Not that I'd expect a teacher to have a clue who I'm friends with. Not a teacher who isn't Mrs Jarman, anyway. If she were here then she'd sort this out.*

"Aren't you the lucky one!" says Mr Kennedy, giving her a big smile. "Most people only get to be with one friend but you've got three in your cabin. Now you'd better collect your bag and hurry up before they've chosen all the best beds!"

Tally stares at him. How can he think that she's lucky? There is nothing lucky about any of this.

"Off you go then!" says Miss Perkins, her face twisted into a tight smile. "Let's not start the week by making a fuss about nothing, hey?"

Tally knows all about making a fuss and what she is doing right now is definitely *not* it. Her head starts to make the buzzing sound that it always does when she gets upset, and for a brief moment she imagines what would happen if she let the meltdown happen. What would Mr

Kennedy and Miss Perkins do if they could see exactly how they are making her feel?

Swallowing hard, she clenches her fists and digs her fingernails into the palms of her hands. It hurts but it's not as bad as the panic that is worming its way through her veins when she thinks about sleeping in the same cabin as the other girls.

"Let's give it a go with your friends in Cabin One," says Mr Kennedy, giving her a slightly worried look. "They *are* your friends, aren't they?"

Tally opens her mouth and then closes it again and nods. How can she even begin to explain? She can't stand here and tell the head of year seven that the girls *aren't* her friends because friends should accept you for who you are and don't betray you when it suits them. And the reason she can't tell him that is because it's not what he wants to hear. He wants her not to be a problem and *not being a problem* is what Tally spends most of her time trying to do.

Even when it half destroys her.

Slowly, she picks up her bag and walks away down the path with the puddles of sunlight, right to the end where she can see a row of little cabins. She walks past all of them until she reaches the last one and then, taking a deep breath, she tightens her grip on her bag and pushes the door open.

"Tally!" Layla rushes over to greet her. "How great is it that we're all together again? This week is going to be so brilliant!"

"Hi, Tally." Lucy is standing behind Layla. "Welcome to Cabin One!"

"The best cabin!" calls a familiar voice, and when Tally peers over Layla's shoulder she sees Ayesha, giving her a big grin. They've obviously forgotten about last week's drama lesson and how angry Lucy was with her for telling everyone that she used to like Luke.

"I kept you a top one," Layla tells her, gesturing towards a set of bunk beds. "I know you like being up high. I'm on the bed beneath you."

Tally steps forward into the cabin. As well as the three other girls, the room has three sets of bunk beds and a girl who she's never seen before.

"This is Skye," Lucy tells her, stepping to one side. "She's from Redhill High and she's savage!"

"All right?" The girl called Skye gives Tally a disinterested glance and then returns to what she was doing. Which, from where Tally is standing, appears to be texting, but that can't be right because Mr Kennedy was very firm about how GoCamp bans all electronic devices from the site.

Tally walks slowly across the room to the empty bed and then turns to look at Layla.

"Is this one mine?" she checks, quietly.

Layla nods and walks across to where Tally is standing. "Unless you'd rather swap with me and have the bottom bunk? I don't mind either way."

Tally shakes her head and throws her bag up on to the bed. She always sleeps better if she's somewhere high up and, even though she's sure that she isn't going to be able to sleep for even one minute while she's here, it's kind of nice that Layla was thinking about her.

"I'm so glad that we're together," Layla whispers as the other girls start talking. "I wrote your name on my piece of paper."

"What do you mean?" Tally pauses, one hand on the ladder.

"I chose you as my friend," Layla says, sounding nervous. "I just want everything to go back to how it used to be. I've really missed you. Was that OK?"

Inside Tally's head she is screaming. *No. That was not OK. She was supposed to be with her actual friend, not stuck here with girls who don't really know her. And she is never going back to how things used to be – absolutely not.*

Layla looks at her anxiously.

"It's OK," Tally tells her. "I guess." Then she climbs up the ladder and the bed and sits cross-legged on the mattress. She doesn't like this one bit but she doesn't have to hurt Layla's feelings. Opening her bag, she pulls out her journal and quietly starts to write while the other girls start to organize their beds, making the cabin buzz with noise.

"I'm starving," announces Lucy, once her bed is made. "I hope they ring the bell for lunch soon."

"I wonder what we'll be given to eat?" says Layla. "My cousin stayed here last year and he said that the food was lush."

"I wouldn't hold your breath." The girl called Skye looks up. "I've done loads of these activity weeks and the food is always atrocious. It's a money-saving thing – they charge our parents a ton of cash and then feed us slops so that they can make a profit."

The room is quiet for a moment and then Lucy laughs. "It sounds like you know what you're talking about."

"What's your friend called?" asks Ayesha, pointing to the bed across from Tally's and it's only now that Tally realizes that there is someone else in the cabin. She's lying down with her back to the room and is so still that she must be asleep.

"She's not my friend." Skye's words are sharp. "My stupid school messed up and put me with her. I think there's something wrong with her — she's not got any friends and she's always being sent to the isolation room at school."

There's an awkward silence as the girls all stare up at the top bunk.

"Is she dangerous then?" whispers Ayesha, looking worried. "It's only the violent kids that get sent to isolation at our school."

Skye laughs and stretches out on her bed. "Dangerous? No way. Unless you think that a complete obsession with cats is dangerous. Seriously, she spends most break-times wandering around making miaowing noises. She thinks she *is* a cat."

There is a sharp edge to her words that makes Tally shiver.

Layla unzips her bag and pulls out her pyjamas.

"I'm going to start unpacking," she says loudly, shooting a quick glance up at Tally. "Maybe we should all choose which cupboard we're going to put our stuff in?"

"I've already put my things in this one," says Skye, flinging her arm in the direction of the biggest cupboard.

"You guys can choose from the others."

Tally sweeps her gaze around the small room. Other than the cupboard that Skye has claimed, there are four smaller cupboards. So five cupboards and six people. The biggest one is obviously supposed to be used by two people.

"I'll have this one," says Lucy, opening the one closest to her bed. "Ayesha, you should take the one next to me."

"Which means that Tally and I can have these two," says Layla, taking a pile of socks over to the cupboards nearest the door. "That works perfectly."

They all start unpacking their things, Skye doing most of the talking while Lucy and Ayesha hang on to her every word. Layla is busy with her bag and the room fills with noise so nobody notices when the girl in the top bed rolls over and opens her eyes.

Nobody except Tally, lying in the bunk opposite her.

The girl blinks slowly and stares at Tally. Beneath them, the girls surge past and head towards the door.

"We're going to see what's outside," Lucy calls to Tally. "Are you coming?"

Tally pauses, her mind working fast. "In a minute."

Layla closes her cupboard and looks up at Tally with concern on her face. "I'll wait for you."

None of them notice that the silent girl is listening to every word. It's like she's invisible or they've forgotten that she's even there.

"I just need some time to unpack," Tally tells Layla, shaking her head. "I'll come out when I'm done."

Layla gives Tally another quick glance and then smiles. "OK," she says. "Come and find us when you're ready."

The girls pile out through the door, and even when it's closed, Tally can still hear Skye telling the others about which people are the most popular and which people they should be avoiding from Redhill High. She waits until the voices have faded and then quickly finishes her journal entry before looking at the girl lying across from her.

"Hi," she says quietly. "My name's Tally."

The girl blinks again, as if she's surprised that Tally has seen her, but says nothing.

"What's your name?" asks Tally.

"I'm Jade," says the girl, her voice so quiet that Tally has to strain to hear her. "And I don't think that I'm a cat."

Tally smiles at her. "Of course you don't."

"I heard what Skye said," Jade whispers. "But I'm not stupid. I just like cats, that's all."

"I prefer dogs," Tally tells her. "But cats are OK, I guess."

"Cats are awesome!" Jade sits up and turns to face

Tally, a shy smile tugging at her mouth. "Did you know that cats can cure themselves of illness by purring? It's something to do with the vibration and the best frequency for healing. Isn't that amazing?"

"That *is* amazing," says Tally. "I wish that humans could do that."

Jade giggles. "How do you know that we can't? Have you ever tried making a purring noise when you're feeling upset or hurt, because I have and I can tell you, it definitely makes me feel a lot better."

Tally grins. "I actually think that sounds really good," she tells her. "Sometimes I—"

A distant bell rings and the door crashes open as the girls pour back in.

"Tally! They've rung the bell for lunch!" calls Layla. "Let's walk over together and then we can all sit at the same table."

Eating in the canteen at GoCamp has been one of the things that Tally has been dreading the most. If it's anything like the canteen at school, then it's going to be full of the things she finds difficult. Noise and people and just too much. She thought that she'd be able to go in with Aleksandra, but as that's clearly not going to happen, she'd far rather be with Layla and the others than have to go in alone.

"OK," she says, lowering herself down to the floor. "But what about Jade?"

"Who?" asks Lucy, looking confused.

Tally points up to the other bed, where Jade is sitting as still as she possibly can, almost like she's trying not to be seen.

"Is *that* her name?" sniffs Skye, storming past. "We all just call her *Kitty*."

"That's not kind," Tally tells her. "Names like that can really hurt."

Skye pauses and looks Tally up and down.

"Whatever. But just a quick word of advice? If you start hanging around with Cat Girl then nobody else is going to want to be anywhere near you. So make your choice."

Tally's stomach lurches, just like it did on the coach when they were going round the twisty bends. Skye is being horrible and Tally knows all about how it feels to be spoken about like you don't matter.

"I'm going for lunch," announces Skye. "Who's coming with me? I'll introduce you to Khloe. She's my best friend and you're going to love her! She's hilarious plus her mum works in the music industry and she always has spare tickets for gigs!"

There's a brief pause. Lucy and Ayesha give each other a quick glance and then nod.

"We're coming," Lucy says. "And so is Layla."

"I'm doing whatever Tally wants to do," says Layla, her voice a bit shaky.

Tally looks at her. Her previous best friend in the whole world is staring at her with big eyes. Tally knows that Layla wants her to go with them, and she also knows that she is trying really hard to make things better with her. That should count for something, right?

Skye flings the door open and then looks back over her shoulder, a smirk on her face.

"You can sit with us and have a great week being popular or you can choose *Kitty* and be miserable and alone. It's up to you."

I don't want to be alone. I really, really don't. I don't think I can do this week if I'm all on my own and fake-friends are better than no friends, surely?

The words flood through Tally's head and she wants to stamp her feet and yell. Why is this happening? It's completely unfair. She was supposed to be eating lunch with Aleksandra, not being forced into choosing between being with people or being alone.

Her eyes flicker up towards the bed, and she tells

herself that if Jade gives her even the tiniest sign that she wants her to stay then she'll tell the rest of them to go on without her and will wait for the other girl.

But Jade isn't sitting up any more. Instead, she's lying down with her back to the room again and Tally has no way of knowing *what* it is that she might want. Perhaps she just wants them all to go away and leave her in peace? Tally knows how it feels to need to be on your own sometimes.

"Tally? Shall we go?" Layla's voice breaks through Tally's thoughts. Tally sees that even though the others have already left, Layla is standing by the door.

Waiting for her, like a real friend.

Telling herself that it's the right thing to do, Tally nods and follows Layla out of the cabin. Her stomach is still squirming, but she squashes the feeling away. Even if it isn't the *right* thing to do, it's the only thing that she *can* do.

There isn't really a choice to make.

Date: Monday 15th June.

Situation: Arriving at camp.

Anxiety rating: 9. And believe me when I tell you that an anxiety rating this high at home would mean an instant meltdown. But I'm here with everyone and I can't let my true feelings out, so instead they're all bottled up, eating away at me from the inside like nasty little insects.

Dear Diary,

So yet again everything has gone wrong. So many things that I'm not even going do a dramatic listing of everything as camp would probably be over by the time I'd finished. Even my Worry Window is going to have to change times to fit in with camp, but I have some free time now while everyone unpacks their stuff, so here goes. The main problem is that Aleksandra decided to abandon me for a tent and another friend. Well, I don't know if it was intentional, but it hurt as much as if it was. When I got the dreadful news I felt like I had been punched in the stomach. This sort of thing might not matter so much to others but for me it is catastrophic. It's not only a massive change in what I had expected to happen, but I have to face that change without the friend that makes me feel safe in these situations. And nobody even seems to realize how difficult this is for me. The teachers just chivvied me along in that way that some teachers do. I hate being chivvied. It's patronizing but I think it's also really rude. In fact I'd go so far as to say it's actually dangerous because it's teaching me to ignore what I'm really feeling. Here's how it goes:

Step 1: I feel really anxious about something, so I explain that I can't do that thing, or I say what I need in order to be able to do it. My mum calls this *making my needs known*, and says I must try and do it politely, so I do.

Step 2: The adult automatically assumes I'm just trying to be difficult. Why is this? Like I don't have enough things I feel really anxious about on a daily basis without HAVING TO MAKE THEM UP?! (Actually, even my mum does this sometimes – so what hope do I have if the person who knows me best of all thinks this about me?)

Step 3: The adult's face or body language usually shows some form of frustration, which instantly raises my anxiety levels further.

Step 4: The chivvying starts. "Go on, you can do it, it's only..." etc. etc.

Step 5: Now if it's my family the extra stress of having to argue with them instantly gets converted into anger and they pretty quickly get the picture that this is not me just trying to get out of something. It's what I call a "can't" not a "won't". However, with school and the outside world the rules are different. At school, I feel I have to try to contain all that stress and anger and try again, calmly, to make my point and explain my situation. What do I get in return? I'll tell you. I get step 6.

Step 6: The chivvying goes up a notch. This usually involves them telling me how I feel: "But you like so and so, last week you were fine..." etc. etc.

Step 7: I continue to try and explain that that may have been how I felt last week, but this week I feel like this. How can anyone else know how I feel better than me, after all?

Step 8: The adult's patience has gone and we are now in slightly angry territory. I have two options here:

   a. Give up, and force myself to do whatever it is they want of me.

   b. Go into meltdown. Well, calling B an option is

wrong actually, because if I have got to meltdown stage it definitely is not a choice. At all costs I will try and avoid that in public for obvious reasons, so of course I usually give in to option A.

Step 9: The adult now believes that when I tell them I can't do something or I need something changed, all they have to do is keep persuading and coaxing and CHIVVYING me and I will get over it.

What they are actually doing is telling me that what I feel doesn't matter. I think they are basically saying, "Stop making a fuss and just fit in, will you, instead of making our lives difficult." They don't say it, but I know they think it. How am I meant to be able to stick up for myself and say what I need when I'm older if no one will listen to me now?

I literally cannot wait until I'm old enough to make my own decisions. Though Nell says that life is never like that even for adults. She says I can't go to my boss when I get a job and just say, "Sorry, but I'm not doing that." Little does Nell know that won't happen, because I'LL be the boss!

By the way, in case anyone is interested, here is what you should do in that situation. It's so simple. Just ask me what it is that is causing my stress, and once we work out what it is, then ask me what will help me feel better in the situation. Often when we can come up with solutions together, it means I can end up doing whatever it is that is needed of me. See? Simple, isn't it?

CHAPTER 8

Inside the canteen, the noise is everywhere and no matter how hard she tries to block it out, Tally can feel the panic bubbling up inside her. She tries to squash it back into place, but she knows from experience that it won't stay down for long. Panic is a bit like one of her squishies – she can squidge it and push it but eventually it has to spring back up.

Aleksandra comes into the canteen a few minutes after they've sat down and waves excitedly when she sees Tally, but there are no empty seats at the table where they're sitting and so Aleksandra ends up on the far side of the room with Mina. Tally tries not to mind but it isn't easy.

"HEY!" The yell from the table next to them is sudden and shocking and it takes Tally completely by surprise. "CAN YOU PASS THE WATER?"

Skye rolls her eyes. "That's Gregory. You're probably going to be hearing a lot about him this week. Or a lot *of* him, anyway – he's the noisiest, most annoying person on the planet, so keep your fingers crossed that he isn't in your team. He can't concentrate on anything for more than two seconds at a time and he gets *everything* wrong."

"CAN I JUST GET THE—"

Too loud! Tally slumps her shoulders and tries to remember the breathing pattern that Mum showed her for times like this. Breathe in slowly and count to four. Hold your breath and count to four. Breathe out slowly and count to four. Repeat. Repeat. Repeat.

But the table next to them erupts with noise and Tally loses her focus.

"Gregory!"

"Why did you do that?"

"My legs are covered in water now, you idiot."

They all look over at the kids next to them. Two are mopping water off the table while another frantically dabs her trousers with paper napkins. Someone else is rescuing the food that is in danger of getting soaked while the fifth just sits there, munching away on his cheese sandwich as if he has no idea of the chaos that he has caused.

"He gets everything wrong," repeats Skye, picking up

her glass. "It doesn't matter how many times he gets told off. He never changes."

One of the teachers walks across the room.

"What happened here?" he asks, stopping in between the two tables.

"Gregory," answers the girl with wet trousers. "Gregory happened, as usual. It's all his fault, Mr Limpkin."

The teacher glares down at the boy in front of him.

"Do you remember what we told you before coming on this trip?" he demands. "Any of your daft behaviour and you'll be going straight back home."

Gregory looks up at him. "I just wanted some water," he says. "Nobody would pass it to me so I had to get it myself."

"That's strike one," warns Mr Limpkin, ignoring him. "Any more issues with you and I'll be phoning your dad."

Gregory scowls and looks down at the table and the teacher moves away.

"I told you," says Skye. "Total nightmare."

As soon as everyone has finished eating, a woman stands up at the front of the room and raises her hand for silence.

"Hello, everyone, and welcome to GoCamp!" she says, smiling. "We're really glad that you're all here and we've got an action-packed time ahead of us. In a moment you're going to be split into groups and sent off for your first activity, but before that, I'd like to introduce the rest of the team." She points towards the door where a group of people are standing. "First we have Kirsten – she's the leader for Team Phoenix."

Kirsten steps forward, her eyes roaming around the room. "Welcome to GoCamp," she says. "The one thing I ask from my team is that you give one hundred and ten per cent. When things seem hard and the going gets tough, I want you to dig deep and find your inner strength. And in return, I'll make sure that this is five days of your life that you'll never forget. If you're in my team then you're in the winning team!"

She steps back into line and a murmur spreads around the room. Tally crosses her finger tightly underneath the table. Kirsten sounds absolutely terrifying and she really, really hopes that she isn't in her group.

The first woman laughs. "So, one thing I need to mention is that this week has a competitive aspect and, as you can see, Kirsten takes that very seriously! Each group will score points on every activity and, at the end of the week, the group with the winning score will be given the GoCamp Award for best team."

She nods towards the door again and a man steps forward, giving a quick grin.

"My name is Drew and I'm the leader for Team Basilisk. I'm sure you're all going to get a lot from your time here and while the main aim is to challenge yourself, the point of the competition is to build some good team spirit. So, as well as getting points for how quickly or effectively you complete each activity, there are points up for grabs for working well with each other and encouraging other members of your group. Because after all, everyone wants to win, don't they?"

Everyone mutters their agreement except Gregory, the boy at the next table. He starts cheering and whooping until he sees Mr Limpkin giving him the teacher death-glare, when he stops abruptly. Tally looks down at the table. She isn't sure that she's going to be able to do any of the activities herself, never mind help anyone else to do them. If Mrs Jarman were here then she'd be giving her their agreed thumbs-down signal and asking to go somewhere quiet and away.

The introductions continue and Tally zones them out. She can't do this. It was a massive mistake to think that she could. She's only been away from home for half a day and she's already exhausted with having to put on her "I'm

OK" face for so long. There is absolutely no way that she can stay here until Friday.

"*He* doesn't look old enough to work here," whispers Layla, nudging Tally in the arm and pulling her attention back into the room. "He looks like he's the same age as my brother."

Tally glances where she's pointing and sees a teenage boy stepping forward, looking a bit nervous.

"And lastly," says the woman at the front, "I'd like to introduce you to Jack. He finished school last year and he's working here to get some experience before he heads off to university in September."

"Hi, everyone." Jack gives a little wave to the room. "So yeah – I'm Jack and I'm the leader of Team Minotaur, as well as being responsible for the animals here at the centre."

Tally's head snaps up and she gives Jack her full attention. Nobody has said anything about animals before.

"We've got an amazing animal sanctuary over in the west field," he continues, sounding more confident now. "We rescue animals that nobody else wants and try to rehome them. At the moment we've got a dog, some chickens and a couple of guinea pigs as well as a few other guests. I can always do with some help, so whenever

135

you've got some free time you're very welcome to come and hang out in the Sanctuary."

"Yeah, right! Like we've come here to help clean out some abandoned animals!" whispers Skye. "Nobody wants them for a reason."

Tally is struck with two very powerful thoughts. The first is that she has every intention of spending as much time as possible at the animal sanctuary.

The second is that she definitely does not like Skye. Not one little bit.

Tally's mind is so full of the possibility of helping look after the animals that she pays no attention to anything else that is said. It's only when Layla taps her on the arm that she realizes that everyone is standing up and moving outside.

"We've got to get into our teams now," Layla tells her. "I wish we were together but at least we get to see each other later in the cabin."

Tally stares at her blankly and Layla laughs.

"You didn't hear a word that they said, did you? I'm in Team Basilisk so I'm rock climbing this afternoon, but you're in Team Phoenix so you have to head over to the bay for raft building. You've got Lucy with you, so you won't be all on your own."

They reach the doors and Layla points towards the trees. "Just follow that path. Your team are meeting each other when you get there."

A group of people stream past them and Tally is swept up in their midst. There's no time to wonder if she can just go and hide in the cabin because her feet are moving and then the bay is appearing before her. And suddenly she's breathing a little more calmly without even trying.

"Welcome to Team Phoenix," says Kirsten, appearing in front of them. "Your first activity is going to test your cooperative skills and ability to communicate with each other, as well as your aptitude for solving problems. You will be competing against Team Minotaur in this task. The first team to build a raft and paddle out to bring back one of the flags that are currently in the middle of the bay will be the winners."

Tally looks at the people standing around her, her heart sinking when she sees Ameet and Skye talking to Lucy. There are a couple of kids from the other school who she's never seen before and then, standing a little way away from the rest of them is Jade. Someone has obviously made her leave the cabin and join in. So that makes seven of them in total.

"Don't start without me!" yells a voice and then a boy hurls himself into the centre of the group.

Skye groans loudly. "Not *another* useless person on our team." She shoots a sneaky glance at Jade and then her eyes flash towards Tally. "It's totally unfair."

"You must be Gregory," says Kirsten. Tally can't tell if she didn't hear Skye's comments or if she is just choosing to ignore her. "Punctuality is very important when you're working as a team, you know?"

Gregory shrugs. "I got lost," he tells her. "All the trees look the same, don't they?"

"Anyway," says Kirsten, looking at the rest of them. "There are two main rules for this task. You can only use the equipment provided and every single member of the team must be on the raft for its voyage into the bay. No man left behind, that's our motto in Team Phoenix!"

"Or woman," adds Gregory. "We shouldn't leave any women behind either."

Kirsten gives him a look and then nods at Jack, the leader of Team Minotaur, who has been briefing his team over by the shoreline.

"Don't forget, you're going to have to work together if you want to beat the other team. So good luck and off you go!"

Gregory dashes towards the equipment that is piled up for their group, with Skye, Ameet, Lucy and the two other girls close behind him. Tally looks across at Jade and gives her a smile, but Jade either ignores her or doesn't notice and Tally has no choice but to walk across to where everyone else is gathered, her hands flapping at her side as she tries to figure out what she's supposed to do now.

"What's wrong with *her*?" Tally hears Skye ask Lucy. "I saw her doing that weird twitching thing at lunchtime too. It makes her look like Kitty when she does that."

Tally stares at her feet and forces her hands to stay still. She hears Lucy say, "She's not really weird. She's just—"

"We need to put this barrel over here!" yells Gregory with perfect timing, grabbing one of the plastic tubs. "Come on! Hurry up!"

Tally looks up, relieved by his interruption. She may have only met Skye an hour ago but she already knows that it is massively important that she doesn't find out about the real Tally. Not from Lucy, anyway. Tally has met people like Skye before and they don't like anything that is different to them. And they definitely think that being autistic is *different*.

If Tally wants any chance of not spending the next few days on her own, then she cannot allow herself to be autistic. Not where people can see her, anyway. But the problem with this is that autism is not like a tap. She can't just turn it off when she wants to.

Ameet shakes his head. "Hang on a minute. We need to work out how big the raft has to be first. We have to fit everyone on to it."

"Yeah." Lucy walks towards the wooden planks. "I reckon we can probably fit four of us on each plank, so we need two planks."

"Which means that the barrel *can't* go where Gregory wants it," adds Skye, putting her hands on her hips. "We'll definitely sink if it goes there. It was a stupid idea."

"Just get a move on!" yells Gregory, looking desperately over at Team Minotaur. "We have to win!"

"I don't really want to do this," whispers Jade, making Tally jump. Jade has crept up behind her. "Did you know that cats hate the water because it makes their coats heavy and that makes them feel that they can't escape as fast as they want to?"

"I know a cat who likes dipping its paws into a pond though," Tally says, thinking about Bugsy, the cat who lives next door to them. "So not all cats hate water."

Jade nods. "That's because *that* cat has *chosen* to go near the water," she explains. "Cats hate surprises. They like being in control."

Tally wonders if it's possible for cats to have Pathological Demand Avoidance, like her. It makes sense. She can do lots of things when she feels in control. The problems only start when she feels overwhelmed and heavy with what everyone else wants her to do, a bit like a cat's fur must feel like if they go into water. Maybe she and cats are the same – they just want to spring away from any demands.

"You two can untangle this rope!" calls Skye, throwing it across to where Tally and Jade are standing. "Do something useful, why don't you?"

Untangle it yourself! The words scream out in Tally's head, but she clamps her lips closed and traps them inside her mouth. Skye already thinks that she's different. Getting angry about being given an instruction is not going to help her right now.

Jade picks the rope up and sits down on the sand, starting to work on the knots. Tally pauses for a second. She could sit down and join Jade, but she knows what's happening here. Skye has seen Jade talking to Tally and decided that Tally has made her choice. And now she's punishing Tally for choosing Jade, which is totally unfair because she didn't ask Jade to start a conversation with her and she shouldn't be left out just because she's being friendly.

Tally's head starts its familiar buzzing. She thought she'd got past caring whether other kids actually liked her or not. She isn't daft – it's not like she's suddenly Little Miss Popular since everyone at school found out about her autism. Things can still be really tricky – but at least they don't make fun of her any more.

Not to her face, anyway.

The buzzing gets louder and Tally blinks hard, trying to stay in control. She wants to tell Skye that she, Tally, is an excellent friend and that if Skye would just give her a chance and get to know her then she'd see all the great things about her. She just wants Skye to see her, which is very confusing when really, she knows that Skye isn't actually very nice. But this week isn't about *nice*. It's about survival and not being alone, and so she's going to have to do whatever it takes to be part of the group. "There's no point in trying to impress her," says Jade and when Tally looks down, she sees the other girl staring up at her. "You can't win against people like her. It's us against them and *they* always win."

Tally stares down at Jade.

"What do you mean? Who are '*us*'?"

Jade hands her the end of the rope. "You know. It must

be the same in your school? There are the kids who have everything and then there are the rest of us. We have to exist so that *they* can be *them*. They're on the inside and we're on the outside. That's just the way it works, especially for kids like us."

Tally shakes her head, partly to clear the buzzing sound and partly to make Jade stop talking because her words are not helping. Not one little bit. Tally thinks that in retrospect, it was better when Jade wasn't talking at all.

"No." She glares at Jade and throws the rope onto the sand. "I'm not part of your '*us*', OK?"

She moves away from the other girl and hovers on the edge of the group, trying to figure out a way to get involved.

"Tally!" Lucy waves her across to join them. "Can you hold this barrel in place while we tie it down?"

Tally nods gratefully and rushes across to where Lucy and Skye are standing. This is her chance to fit in. All she has to do is not flap her hands or do anything unexpected and pretend that she's just the same as they are. She's got this. Nobody is more of an expert at hiding parts of herself than Tally is.

"How lame does that animal sanctuary sound?" says Skye, leaning across the barrel.

"So lame," agrees Lucy. "I thought he was at least

going to say that they had some interesting animals, not a couple of boring guinea pigs and a stray dog."

Skye looks at Tally and she realizes that she's supposed to be joining in.

"So lame," she repeats, but her voice sounds flat. It's hard to be animated about something when you're telling a massive lie and Tally hates lying more than anything else.

She holds on to the barrel until it is in place. Lucy and Skye move over to the other side of the raft but they don't say anything to Tally and she isn't really sure whether she's supposed to follow them or stay out of the way. She stands back and watches as they all bicker and squabble and argue about how to stop the raft from falling apart. Gregory is wildly yelling his ideas, but Ameet, Lucy and Skye take control and pay no attention to him. Eventually he stomps across to where Tally is standing and heaves a giant sigh.

"It's all *wrong*," he tells her, his voice furious. "The barrels need to be more towards the end if we don't want to capsize."

Tally shrugs and steps away. It's bad enough that the cat-loving, not-speaking girl somehow thinks that they're the same. The last thing she needs is loud, annoying Gregory latching on to her too. She doesn't stand a chance of surviving this week if all the *different* kids think that she's one of *them*.

"Maybe we should get Kitty to try the raft out first!" Skye's voice rings across the sand. "Cats have nine lives after all, so if it sinks then she'll be fine!"

Tally looks across to see Skye pointing at Jade and then throwing her arm around Lucy's shoulder. Ameet grins and the other two girls start sniggering. Jade's face flushes a deep red and she stares down at the rope, her fingers speeding up as she works harder at one of the knots.

Tally's heart thumps in her chest and she wonders if she should say something. But then she remembers Jade's comment about them being on the outside and she clenches her mouth tightly closed. She desperately wants to be on the inside where it's warm and happy and safe.

Doesn't everyone?

"It's time to launch!" yells Ameet. "We all need to put on a lifejacket and then carry the raft into the water!"

Someone passes Tally a buoyancy aid and she straps it on, trying to stop her hands from shaking. This is the part that she's been dreading. It's not that she's afraid of being in the water – she's an excellent swimmer, she knows that. It's being out on the raft with the rest of them that bothers her. There are no choices once they're out in the middle of the bay. She can't decide that she's changed her mind and go somewhere quiet.

It's all or nothing.

Looking around, Tally sees two teachers coming towards them. If one of them were Mrs Jarman, like it was supposed to be, then right now Tally would definitely be telling her that she needs a time-out. But it isn't Mrs Jarman. It's Miss Perkins with Mr Limpkin, the teacher from Redhill High. And Miss Perkins does not care even one little bit if Tally's head is buzzing or her stomach is swirling. Miss Perkins only cares that everyone is doing exactly what they're supposed to be doing.

"Let's go!" shouts Skye. "Team Minotaur are already in the water!"

There's a rush of feet and Tally is propelled forward along with everyone else. Someone pushes her towards the raft, and before she can even figure out the words to explain that she *can't do it*, she's in the water and perched on one of the wooden planks at the back of the raft with two paddles in her hands and Jade sitting in front of her.

And she *is doing it*.

"Hurry up, Gregory!" yells Ameet, his head swivelling to look at the opposing team. "They've all fallen into the water – we've got a chance to overtake them if we get going right now!"

Tally looks at the shoreline. Gregory is standing with his feet planted firmly apart and a militant look on his face.

"No! I'm not coming," he shouts. "You wouldn't listen to me and you've made a stupid raft that is going to sink."

Tally isn't sure that she's ever met anybody who gets so angry, so quickly.

"Come on, Gregory." Kirsten appears behind him. "This is the fun bit!"

"No way." His face wrinkles in outrage. "You can't make me."

"The whole team needs to be on the raft," Kirsten reminds him. "Otherwise it won't count."

"This is so typical," moans Skye, from the front of the raft. "We do all the work and he messes it up, *just for a change*. He's such a pain."

The two teachers walk up to where Gregory is standing, and from the looks on their faces, they are not impressed.

"What's the problem here?" calls Mr Limpkin.

"Gregory is the problem!" yells Skye. "He's being crazy, *as usual*."

"Seriously? We've not even been here for half a day and you're already causing trouble." Mr Limpkin glares at Gregory. "Just get on the raft."

"No." Gregory glares back but Tally can see that his legs are shaking and his breathing has sped up. And it suddenly hits her like a bolt of lightning.

Gregory isn't angry.

Gregory is *scared*.

Mr Limpkin's face contorts in displeasure.

"Get on the raft or I'll be straight on the phone to your dad," he tells Gregory, his voice carrying across the water. "And I think we both know just how delighted he's *not* going to be when I tell him that he has to leave work *and* sort a sitter for your sister and then get down here to collect you."

Tally holds her breath as waves of emotion wash over Gregory's face. And then, with one last kick of the sand, he grabs the lifejacket that Kirsten is holding out and pulls it over his head before wading out to the raft and sitting on the plank across from Tally.

"Now let's go!" screams Ameet. "Go! Go! Go!"

Tally passes Gregory a paddle and then dips hers into the water. The next few minutes are a blur of activity as everyone paddles and shouts and the water sloshes over them.

"Everyone paddle harder!" screeches Lucy. "We're gaining on Team Minotaur!"

Tally glances across at Gregory. His face is pale and his eyes are closed and his paddle is very, very still.

"It's OK," she whispers, although the rest of the team are making so much noise that she really doesn't need to bother trying to be quiet. "You're safe, you know. The life jacket will keep us afloat if we fall in."

Gregory opens his eyes and looks at her.

"But it won't help us if the raft capsizes and traps us underneath, will it? Or if there are sharks in the water or there's a freak lightning storm and we get hit because being on the water is just about the worst place to be, did you know that?"

Tally swallows hard. She's already got a list of worries as long as her arm. She doesn't really need Gregory adding to them.

"And I can swim OK in the swimming pool," he continues, his breathing speeding up. "But I've never swum in the sea before and there could be a riptide or an undertow or something and I might not be strong enough to beat it. And then I might float out into the open water and starve to death before anyone can find me."

His eyes are wide and his hands are clenching the paddle so tightly that his knuckles are white. He pants in and out, like he's gasping for breath, and part of Tally wants to turn away and get back to paddling so that this whole ordeal can be over as quickly as possible.

But she knows what a meltdown looks like and she knows how it feels to be scared. And she also knows what makes her feel a bit better when those things are happening to her. She's not about to start going on about her Worry Window to this boy who she doesn't even know, but that doesn't mean that she can't help him out a bit.

"You're right," she tells Gregory. "Bad things *can* happen. They happen all the time."

He snaps his head around and looks at her, his face alarmed.

"What? But I—"

"Just listen," she says. "Bad things *can* happen but they aren't particularly likely to happen to us today. But just in case, let's work out what you can do about it."

Gregory stares at her. "What are you on about?"

Tally fixes him with a firm look. "If the raft capsizes and you get stuck underneath, then you can just pull yourself along until you reach the edge. It might be a bit frightening but you'd survive. And there aren't any sharks in this country that would eat us, OK? So we don't need to find a solution to that worry."

"How do you know?"

Tally gulps and then decides to tell the truth. "Because I researched that exact thing before we came," she tells him. "I get worried about stuff too."

"Fine." Gregory sounds reluctant. "But there are all those other things. You can't tell me that *they* aren't real."

"They're totally real," agrees Tally. "But I saw the weather forecast for today and there are no storms predicted. And you're right – you could get swept out to sea, but if that happens then I'll make sure that the Search and Rescue Team don't stop looking until they find you, OK?"

Gregory's mouth tugs itself into the tiniest of smiles. "Do you promise?"

Tally nods firmly. "I promise. Now start paddling so that we can get off this raft, because there are scarier things out here than sharks or riptides."

"Start pulling your weight back there!" screams Skye, right on cue. "We're losing!"

Gregory dips his paddle into the water and Tally copies him.

They might be losing to Team Minotaur but at least nobody is going to have a meltdown on the raft, including her. And that feels a lot like winning.

CHAPTER 9

The instant that they reach the shore, Gregory leaps from the raft and pulls off his life jacket. Then he tears up the beach and into the trees before anyone can stop him. The rest of them pull the raft on to the sand, Skye moaning loudly about the fact that they lost. Tally tries to ignore the barbed comments and snide looks that are thrown in her direction.

Kirsten makes them sit on a log and proceeds to make them all listen to her lengthy and critical feedback.

"You weren't working together," she tells them. "You needed to listen to each other more and use each person's strengths."

"Some people don't have any strengths," mutters Skye, looking pointedly at Jade.

"Everyone has something to offer," Kirsten tells her,

frowning. "And until you figure that out then I'm afraid that Team Phoenix is not likely to be taking home the GoCamp Award for best group."

She keeps talking for a while longer and Tally zones out, letting her gaze drift across the bay to where the waves are breaking. She would love to be out there right now, floating on her back and letting the water support her.

"OK." Kirsten finally finishes her lecture and claps her hands. "You can all head up to the Centre now. You'll find pens and paper and envelopes on the tables and your teachers will be waiting for you. You have half an hour to write a letter home to your family."

Everyone groans.

"Why do we have to write letters?" asks Lucy, her nose wrinkled up like she's been asked to do something disgusting. "I've never written a letter in my life."

"That's one of the reasons that you're going to do it now," Kirsten tells her. "Letter-writing has become a lost art, and during your time here, you're going to rediscover it."

"It's stupid," announces Skye, shaking her head. "What are we supposed to write about?"

"Anything you like," says Kirsten. "The journey here or what you had for lunch. Maybe you could write about the raft-building activity? Or how you're feeling, being away from home. It's your letter so you can write whatever you want. They're completely private – the only person who will read it, other than you, is the person who you decide to send it to."

"Why can't we just send an email if it's such a big deal?" asks Ameet. "I hate writing."

Kirsten looks at her watch and gestures to them all to stand up.

"Firstly, because this is a technology-free week and it's pretty impossible to send an email without a technological device of some kind. Secondly, because writing an actual letter is different. You have to really think about what you want to say to the person who will receive it and it's harder to delete your words. Now hurry up and get back to the canteen, otherwise you're not going to have much time."

Still grumbling, everyone heads back up the path towards the main building.

"I'm surprised that they aren't making us send a letter home by pigeon post," says Lucy as they walk through the trees. "I have no idea what I'm going to write to my mum. She isn't going to be interested in what I had for lunch though, I know that."

Tally trails behind, walking as slowly as she dares

without getting left behind. She isn't feeling particularly pleased about the letter writing either. She loves writing in her journal, but that's just for her. She isn't really sure that writing down her feelings on a piece of paper for someone else to read is a sensible idea at all. Even if it is just Mum, Dad and Nell.

"Everyone find a seat," calls Miss Perkins as they enter the room. Tally glances about. Aleksandra is already there and for one brief second Tally's heart lifts as she contemplates spending time with her friend. But then she sees Mina sitting next to her, laughing at something that Aleksandra has just said, and she turns away, ignoring Aleksandra's frantic waving. Her shoulders slump in exhaustion as she plods towards the table where she sat at lunch. It's only day one and she already feels like an unexploded bomb that could go off at any moment. Layla waves at her, which helps a tiny bit, but the canteen is noisy and now she has to walk all the way across the room and she's sure that everyone is looking at her and she doesn't want to start flapping her hands but she can't figure out what she should be doing with her arms and everything is *just so hard.*

"You can stay in here to write your letter," says Mr Kennedy, once everyone is sitting down. "Or you can take your pen, paper and envelope and find somewhere outside to write. You need to seal your letter inside your envelope and write the address on the front and your name on the back so that we can check that they're all here. Then you can put it into this postbag, which I will leave by the door. You have thirty minutes before suppertime and then there will be some free time in your cabins before lights out."

"Shall we just stay in here?" asks Layla, but Tally is already up and grabbing the stuff that she needs.

"I'm going outside," she says and then she dashes for the door, ignoring the laughter coming from Skye that she is fairly sure is directed at her.

The instant that her feet hit the earth, Tally can feel herself start to relax. Inside the canteen it felt like the walls were closing in on her, but out here it's the exact opposite. She pulls in a deep breath of fresh air and then starts to run towards the trees, not caring where she's going as long as it's somewhere far away. She usually hates to run, but today it seems that her feet have forgotten this fact and they pound the ground, moving faster and faster as she charges through the trees, not noticing the twigs catching in her hair and scratching at her legs and not stopping until her lungs are screaming for more air. Only then does she finally slow down, pushing her way between the bushes to reach a small clearing, where she slumps down with her back resting against the trunk of a large tree.

For a few minutes, she just sits and listens. To begin with, all she can hear is the sound of her own breath, but once that settles down, other noises start to filter in. Birds in the branches above. A dog barking from somewhere over to her left. The wind rustling through the leaves and, if she listens hard enough, waves crashing against the rocks.

What she cannot hear is a single other person.

Tally smiles. The clearing is completely enclosed. The branches that stretch overhead are laden with leaves, and if she leans her head back, it's almost like being in a green tent. She's never thought about having a Safe Space that is outside before but this is perfect. And it's all hers. Nobody else has to find out about this place and she can come here whenever she wants to.

But she still has to write this letter and they'll know if she hasn't. Casting her eyes around, she sees a small log a few feet away. She gets up and drags it across to where a large branch has snapped off a tree. Then she sits on the branch and puts her paper on the log, feeling very pleased with her impromptu, outdoor desk.

And then she starts to write.

Dear Mum, Dad and Nell.

She pauses and chews the end of the pen, trying to figure out what to put next. This is actually incredibly hard and she tries to remember what Kirsten told them to write about. It was something about lunch and the coach journey and how they're feeling.

I ate a cheese sandwich at lunchtime but it was the wrong cheese so I had to take it out. And the bread had bits in and I hate that so I had to leave it on the side. The spread was the right kind but it was on the bread so I couldn't eat it.

Tally stops and reads back what she's written, feeling pleased that she's already ticked one thing off the list. Maybe letter writing isn't that tricky after all.

When I was on the coach I thought that I was going to be sick and it was really awful. My stomach was churning and I felt all hot and sweaty. I hope I'm not getting ill because that would be terrible.

There isn't really anything else to say about the coach journey and it's quite boring to write about, so Tally moves on to the next part of her letter.

How I am feeling: tired and sad and lonely and also angry because you lied to me. You said it would be fun but it isn't fun. You said that I could ask for help from Mrs Jarman but she isn't even here. If you wanted me to come on this trip so that I could be the unhappiest girl in the universe then you should be very pleased because it's horrible and I hate it and I'm not with Aleksandra and everyone is mean and unkind. And I actually might drown or starve to death or get washed out to sea by a riptide or eaten by a shark and I want you to know that if that happens then it will all be your fault.

She pauses and rereads her words. If this letter is going to be sent home then she wants to make absolutely sure that Mum and Dad know how she's feeling. It turns out that Kirsten was right – writing a letter to someone really does make you think about what you want to say. If she was at home right now then she'd just be yelling at them and then she'd get upset and start saying stuff that she didn't really mean. This is much better. Writing it down means that she can let her feelings out and not let feeling scared or angry distract her.

She picks up her pen and finishes the letter, signing off with a flourish.

Please give Rupert a very massive hug from me and tell him that you're sorry for sending me away. Make sure he knows that it isn't his fault.
Lots of love, Tally XOXOXO

She reads her letter back to herself and wonders what Mum and Dad will think when they read it. Maybe she shouldn't have said that stuff about being the unhappiest girl in the universe or it being all their fault if she dies. But it's written now, and no way is she going to do it again, so she stuffs it into the envelope and writes her name on the back before sealing it up before heading out of the clearing and back to the Centre to put her letter into the postbag. Mum and Dad might not think it's the best letter that they've ever had but it *is* the very first time she's ever written to them.

They'll probably put it up on the fridge and keep it there for ever.

Suppertime is exactly the chaotic experience that Tally anticipates that it will be. She is handed a plate of macaroni cheese, which she hates, but her stomach has been rumbling since lunchtime and so she forces herself to eat a few bites, feeling very relieved that Mum packed her some bars in her rucksack. They were supposed to be for emergencies, but at this rate she's going to have eaten the lot by Wednesday.

After the meal is over they are all sent back to their cabins to settle in and spend time together before lights out.

"Cabin inspection will be in forty-five minutes," announces Miss Perkins. "I will be checking the girls' cabins and Mr Kennedy and Mr Limpkin will be checking the boys'. We will give marks out of ten, based on tidiness and cleanliness, and the cabin with the most marks by Saturday evening will be given the Best Cabin award."

"We should totally try to win that," says Lucy as they troop back to Cabin Number One. She pushes open the door and then gasps. "Oh no! What's happened in here?"

"What is it?" asks Ayesha, pushing her to one side. "Oh my goodness! Has someone been inside our cabin?"

"Let me see." Skye barges past and marches inside with the other girls close behind her. Tally waits until last and then slowly walks through the door, not sure that she wants to see whatever has sent them all into such a panic.

Inside the cabin, it's a complete mess. Clothes are strewn across the floor and hanging down from one of the top bunks. A large bag lies in the middle of the room, its contents spilling out, and it's hard to take a step without standing on something.

"Whose clothes are these?" asks Ayesha, bending down to pick up a fluffy, yellow jumper. "Who would wear this?"

"Oh, that's mine," says a quiet voice, and when Tally spins round she sees Jade standing in the doorway. "I was going to tidy it up but Kirsten made me go down to join in with the raft building and I didn't get chance."

"Why isn't it all packed away?" asks Lucy, as Jade creeps further into the room and starts to pick up her belongings. "The rest of us sorted our stuff out when we got here."

"I haven't got a cupboard," says Jade, picking up a pair of jeans. "There aren't enough for everyone so my things are going to have to stay in my bag."

"That's the best place for them, if you ask me," states Skye, walking across the room, not seeming to notice that her feet are trampling Jade's clothes.

Not noticing or not caring. Tally thinks that they might

just be the same thing.

"Skye's cupboard is big enough to share," she says helpfully, picking up a pair of socks and handing them to Jade. "It's twice the size of all the others."

Skye shoots Tally a look. It's not *the* look, but it tells Tally in no uncertain terms exactly what Skye thinks of her. And she clearly doesn't think that she is being helpful.

Just do what they do. Try to fit in.

Tally repeats the words to herself and casts an apologetic glance at Jade, who is busy rescuing a white T-shirt that now has Skye's dirty footprint emblazoned across it. Then she climbs up the ladder and lies down on her bed. She doesn't want to say anything else that's going to make Skye get mad at her, but at the same time, she feels bad for Jade. Especially as she's starting to wonder if she might have been a bit harsh on her, down at the bay.

"It's true, Skye," says Lucy. "Your cupboard *is* bigger."

Skye flashes a big smile at Lucy although it's a smile that doesn't make it as far as her eyes.

"Yeah, but it'll get really confusing if we've both got our stuff in the same place," she says. "And you heard what Jade said. She's happy to have her clothes in her bag." She sits down on her bed and looks at Jade. "That's right, isn't it?"

Jade pauses and, for the tiniest of seconds, Tally thinks that she might be about to tell Skye *no*. Because it isn't OK and she can't possibly be happy. It's unfair and it's mean and it's just wrong, and Tally tells herself that if Jade speaks out then she'll back her up. She'll tell Skye to stop being so unkind.

But Jade just nods and says nothing.

"Only if you're sure," adds Skye. "Just make sure that you put your bag under your bed when you've put all your clothes inside otherwise it'll make the room look messy." She grins at Lucy. "Do you want to see what I've got under my pillow?"

She doesn't wait for a response. She reaches her hand under her pillow and pulls out a mobile phone. Lucy and Ayesha squeal and race across the cabin.

"My parents are on a cruise," Skye tells them. "So I need it to stay in touch with them. I texted them the minute we got here to say how rubbish it is and asking them to come and get me."

She activates the screen and scowls. "They haven't messaged me back."

"Maybe there's no signal at sea?" says Lucy. "We went to France last year and the wifi on the ferry was rubbish."

"They've got data," mutters Skye. "They're probably

just really busy."

The cabin is quiet for a moment and then Skye looks up at them all and grins.

"Khloe's got a phone too," she tells them. "We can message her cabin!"

Khloe was sitting at their table in the canteen. As far as Tally can tell, she doesn't do very much other than agree with everything that Skye says and laugh hysterically every time Skye says anything mean about another kid. There was a lot of hysterical laughter.

The three girls huddle on the bed and start sending messages. Layla stands next to Tally's bed and looks up at her.

"Are you doing OK?" she whispers.

Tally twists her head so that she can look down. Not very long ago she would have trusted Layla enough to tell her the truth. But after everything that's happened, she isn't sure that she wants to share how she's feeling.

Especially not when Jade is still scurrying around trying to pick up her things.

"I'm fine," she says. "Just tired. I'm going to sit up here for a bit."

It's kind of the truth. She *is* tired.

Tired of people being cruel just because they can.

Tired of trying so hard to fit in.

Tired of caring what anyone thinks about her.

"Come and look at this!" Ayesha calls to Layla. "It's hilarious!"

Layla hesitates and then walks across to Skye's bed. Jade finishes repacking her bag and shoves it under the bed before clambering up the ladder and flinging herself on top of the mattress.

Tally rolls over on to her front and, as quietly as she possibly can, pulls her journal and pen out from their hiding place under her pillow. Then she starts to write, letting the voices of the other girls wash over her. They can't see what she's doing up here, and while her journal isn't exactly secret, she doesn't want them to know about it.

Miss Perkins comes in after a while to inspect the cabin. When she walks past Tally's bed she pauses and holds something out.

"There was a phone message for you," Miss Perkins tells her. "Earlier on today."

Then she moves away and Tally stares in surprise at the small piece of paper. Whoever took the message has terrible handwriting but she can still make out the words and the name of the person who called. And while she knows that it was very thoughtful of Mrs Jarman to ring up and let her know that she's so sorry that she couldn't be on the trip but that she hopes Tally can remember all the things they talked about and use them to help her if things get a little tricky, it can't possibly make her feel any better. If anything, it just reminds her that the one person at school who properly understands her isn't actually here.

Still, she carefully folds the note up and tucks it inside the pages of her journal and then, when Miss Perkins has gone, she hides the journal under her pillow before climbing down and collecting her wash kit. She leaves the cabin without saying a word and heads slowly towards the bathroom block, enjoying the feel of the cool night breeze on her skin.

Ever since the night Dad got taken to hospital and Rupert went missing, Tally has loved the night-time. She has discovered the magical thing about darkness is that you can be whoever you want to be when it's dark and you don't even need to wear a mask. Even if whoever you want to be is really just yourself. Or maybe a nicer version of yourself who doesn't let bullies get away with treating other people like dirt.

"Where have you been?" asks Layla when Tally eventually returns to the cabin. "I was about to come and look for you."

"I don't need you to baby me," Tally says shortly. "I'm going to bed."

She lies on her bed and tries to get to sleep, but her eyes are open long after the lights have been turned out and Miss Perkins has come in for the third time to threaten Skye, Lucy and Ayesha with getting sent home if they don't stop talking.

She can't even sleep after the others have dozed off because everything is wrong. The mattress on her bed is too lumpy and the pillow smells strange and she can't stand the sound of five other people breathing. Most of all, she is the only person awake and it feels so, so lonely – like she's the only person in the entire world. And so she lies there, staring at the ceiling and listening to an owl outside, wishing more than anything that she could fly away from here and go home.

Date: Still Monday 15th June – night-time.

Situation: In bed, but there's no way I can go to sleep.

Anxiety rating: 8. Which is still very, very high, but is slightly better than earlier – partly because everyone is asleep and so I don't have to talk to them. The irony is that the fact they're all asleep is also one of things making me feel anxious because I hate being the only person awake.

Dear Diary,

It's currently one a.m. and I'm writing this with a torch under the covers in case I get caught. I CANNOT sleep, so have decided to write my diary. So here I am, trying (and failing) to fall asleep in a cabin full of strangers and girls I haven't got on with for the past few months. Great. Not really what I was hoping for when I agreed to take part in this horrendous trip. I can't believe Layla is sleeping just underneath me (I know she's sleeping cos I can hear her noisy mouth breathing which is going to do my head in). It is nice that Layla is actually making quite an effort with me now. Of course Lucy and Ayesha can't keep an effort up for long, they are already being really cringey with how much they are trying to get Skye to like them. It's just weird sharing with two girls from a different school, but what's even stranger is that they are both complete opposites of each other. I think that Jade might actually be OK and she's kind of interesting. Did you know that cats moan when they're angry AND can rotate their ears 180 degrees? Nope, neither did I till I met her.

Skye, however – let's just say that she's a slightly different story, to put it nicely. You know what? I'm just going to be honest. She's a typical mean, rude popular girl. I mean, I would love to ask her what makes her behave the way that she does but I would probably have my head ripped off if I did so that's not really an option.

It's hard, but I've got to protect myself. It's tough out there. Skye gives me a really bad feeling, but if I hang out with her it will make me much more popular and that might make this week a bit easier. I've noticed that popularity sticks like a piece of chewing gum to those who are friends with the cool kids. It's like you gain popularity points by picking someone cool to hang out with. The problem is that girls like Skye often make me feel not very nice about myself. When I'm with her I almost feel tiny even though I'm actually a bit taller than her. It's the way she speaks to me and puts me down. When I first meet people like her I always wonder what makes them like this but, as I said, I wouldn't dare ask them. I, more than anyone else, know that when you're being horrible, there is always more to it than meets the eye – it doesn't just come from nowhere.

CHAPTER 10

"I am *not* doing that." Tally puts her hands on her hips and glares at Kirsten. "No way."

"It's perfectly safe," Kirsten tells her. "You really don't need to worry."

"Is she scared of heights?" asks Skye meanly, rolling her eyes at Lucy. "What a surprise."

"I'm not scared of heights," Tally says quietly. "I *like* being up high."

Skye shrugs. "So put on the harness and climb," she says. "We get points for every member of the team who makes it to the top, and after yesterday's disaster we need all the points that we can get."

"I'm ready!" yells Gregory. He runs towards the cliff wall and launches himself at the rock. "I bet that I can get to the top first!"

"Not without the right safety equipment, you can't," says Kirsten, nodding at the other instructor who has already introduced himself as Pete. He walks across to Gregory and attaches a rope to his harness, before handing him a helmet.

"You can't go anywhere until I go and sort the ropes," he tells him. "Just hold your horses."

"It's not perfectly safe then, is it?" mutters Tally, under her breath. "If we need safety equipment before we can do it."

"Did you know that cats' claws all curve downwards?" says Jade, sidling up next to her. "It makes it easier for them to climb up a tree but it means that they can't climb down headfirst otherwise they'd slip. So they have to back down the tree trunk."

"Yet another fascinating cat fact from Kitty!" announces Skye, doing up her helmet. "Do you have any more scintillating information for us?"

Jade nods. "Actually, I do. Did you know that cats can jump up to six times their length but humans can't even jump double their own height?"

"That's fascinating," drawls Skye, smirking at Ameet. "Tell us another one."

"Did you know that cats are crepuscular?" says Jade.

"*You're* crepuscular," says Ameet and everyone except Tally laughs.

Jade gulps slightly but she pushes on. "It means they're most active at dawn and dusk."

"Oh my god, how do you know *so much*?" says Skye, smiling sweetly at Jade. "It's like you're a Wiki page on cats. I could honestly stand here all day and listen to you."

"Stop it," says Tally, taking a step closer to Jade, but nobody hears her and she doesn't dare to say it again. The air is charged, like there's about to be a storm, and inside Tally's head feels stretched and taut.

"You're incredible." Skye nods her head and grins at Jade. "We're certainly all going to learn a lot you this week. About cats, anyway."

She turns her back on Jade and starts talking to Ameet and Lucy.

"I don't think that she—" Tally starts to say to Jade but she's talking to thin air because Jade has dashed across to the pile of helmets and is busying herself with trying to find one that fits. Tally is just wondering whether she should go after her when Lucy spins round.

"Skye was telling us that there's a plan to sneak out tonight and meet up with Khloe's cabin," she says, excitedly. "We can all take snacks and have a midnight feast in the woods."

Skye scowls at Lucy. "You weren't supposed to tell anyone except Layla and Ayesha," she scolds. "You've already told Tally now so I suppose she's going to have to come, but don't even think about telling Kitty over there."

"I won't!" assures Lucy. "No way! And Tally won't tell her either, will you?"

"She won't if she wants to be part of our group," snarls Skye.

They both stare at Tally and she feels the tight sensation building in her head. One minute ago Skye was making fun of Jade and now she's leaving her out. It's not OK to mess around with someone's feelings like that.

"You won't tell, will you?" repeats Lucy, her voice a bit firmer. "Nobody wants Jade to come. She's weird."

It's that word that does it. The tension in Tally's head snaps and everything starts to unravel, just like the long length of rope that Pete is now dropping over the edge of the rock wall.

"She's not weird." Tally's voice isn't loud but it carries on the breeze and everyone else stops talking. "And you can't go around saying stuff like that. It's not kind and it hurts people's feelings. You're both being really horrible and I don't want anything to do with it."

"You all need to buddy up," calls Kirsten, breaking up the moment. "Get into pairs and then come over here. One of you will climb first and the other will be holding the rope and then you'll swap over, so don't worry – you'll all get to have a go."

Skye and Lucy glare at Tally and then march off together. The two girls from the other school are already paired up and Ameet sighs loudly as he goes to stand next to Gregory, making his displeasure at having to buddy with him known.

"That just leaves us then," says Jade, wandering back across to where Tally is standing as if nothing has happened. "Shall we go together?"

Tally shakes her head.

"I'm not doing this. I can't."

Jade's face falls. "But if you don't do it then they'll make me pair up with one of them." She points at the others. "And I don't think they want to be with me. Please, Tally."

Tally turns and looks at the rock. She wasn't lying earlier when she said that she wasn't afraid of heights. She really isn't. But she *is* afraid of falling.

"Come on, girls!" calls Kirsten. "Which one of you is going to climb first?"

"Do you want *me* to go first?" asks Jade. "I will, if you

want me to. I'm going to pretend that I'm a cat and then there's no way that I can fall."

An image of Dad pops into Tally's head. He said that she could do anything she wants – she just has to choose.

"You know that thing you said about cats' claws?" she whispers, not looking at Jade. "And how they're curved downwards which makes it easier to climb up things?"

"Yes." Jade's voice is as quiet as Tally's.

"Is that the same for tigers?"

There's a pause before Jade replies. "I guess so. They're big cats, after all."

"I'll do it." Tally turns and nods at Jade. "But I need to go first, OK? If I have to wait then I'm probably going to change my mind."

"When you're ready, ladies!" yells Kirsten.

Over by the rock wall, Gregory has already started to climb while a bored-looking Ameet holds the end of the rope. Tally is relieved to see that Pete is back down from the top and is paying close attention to what is happening.

"So we fix the rope here," says Kirsten, feeding it through a loop in Tally's harness. "And then Jade, you're going to let it pull out through your hands as Tally climbs. You need to give her enough rope so that she can move but not so much that she'll fall if she loses her grip on the rock."

She shows Jade what she means and then smiles at Tally.

"You can climb when you're ready," she tells her.

Tally swallows loudly and then puts her foot on to the rock, pushing herself up so that her hands are stretched above her and she's off the ground.

"Good job!" says Kirsten. "Now reach your left foot out to the side and find another foothold."

Tally does as she's instructed and moves further up. On one side of her, Skye is clambering slowly upwards, and on the other, Gregory is nearly at the top. The two other girls are further down with another instructor.

"You can let out a bit more rope," Kirsten tells Jade. "Tally – move your right hand up and across and pull yourself a bit higher."

And she does. She pulls with her hands and pushes with her feet and she keeps on moving up.

Dad was right.

She is brave and fierce and she's not frightened about—

"Argghhhh!" Skye's voice rings out and bounces off the wall, flooding into Tally's ears. "Oh my god!"

Tally glances across and sees Skye dangling in front

of the rock face, suspended above the ground and only held up by the rope. Her face is contorted and she looks absolutely terrified.

"Get me down!" she screams. "I nearly fell off!"

"You were never going to fall," Kirsten calls. "Look! You're fine. Just reach out and grab the rock."

"I want to come down!" Skye screams again, this time her voice even louder. "I nearly *died*!"

Tally can't hear what Kirsten says to this because her head is fizzing in alarm. Kirsten said that it was safe but Kirsten clearly lied because Skye just fell and she nearly died. She grips the rock even harder and presses her face into the wall. This is not OK. This is absolutely not OK.

"Tally! Skye's down now. You're good to climb further!" calls Kirsten but Tally doesn't respond. Instead she freezes in position, not moving a single muscle.

"I'm going to be OK," she mutters under her breath. "I'm going to be OK."

She closes her eyes and puts all her energy into holding on to the rock. She's scared, so scared – and when Tally feels like this then one of three things can happen. She might get angry and fight; she might get panicky and run away; or, if she can't fight or run away, then she might go into shutdown where it's just Tally and her brain, all alone.

And shutdowns are not nice places to be. It's exhausting to only be able to focus on the thing that is scaring her and not feel able to do anything about it.

For a minute or so, she can't think about anything other than not falling off the cliff. There is only her and the rock face and everything else has disappeared. No – not disappeared. She knows that there are people looking up at her and she knows that they are calling to her but it's like she's trapped inside a bubble and she just can't hear them or see them.

But she can't let the shutdown happen now. Whatever it takes, she has to fight because when her brain shuts down, then her body sometimes shuts down too. Last time it happened (which was when their horrible, grumpy next-door neighbour shouted at her for kicking a football into his garden) she went all floppy and tired and had to sleep for two hours, even though it was the middle of the day. She can't do that now. She'll fall off the cliff for sure.

Using every bit of effort that she can summon, Tally cranks her eyes open and blinks, trying to force herself back to the situation.

Kirsten steps closer to the rock face. "If you want to stop then we can lower you down," she shouts up. "But for us to do that then you're going to need to let go."

The words zoom upwards and swirl around Tally's head. If she wasn't so petrified then she would yell back to Kirsten and tell her exactly what she thinks of this very stupid suggestion, but as it is she just clamps her lips together and holds on even tighter. She didn't do any research on the number of rock-climbing related deaths every year, but she has absolutely no intention of adding to whatever that statistic might be. If she doesn't let go then she can't fall, and if she can't fall then she can't die.

"We need to get her down. Pete – you're going to have to go up and get her." Kirsten's voice sounds worried, which just makes Tally cling on even tighter.

"I can't believe that just happened!" screeches Skye. Tally closes her eyes. "Seriously, Lucy! I literally could have been killed."

"It all happened so quickly." Lucy's voice sounds a bit scared. "One minute you were climbing and the next you were just dangling on the end of the rope. You were amazing though – I'd be crying right now if that happened to me."

"I don't cry," scoffs Skye. "Even when I have a near-death experience. Now why is Tally just standing there? Doesn't she know that she's supposed to be going up?"

Breathe in. Breathe out. Tally tries to block out everything except the sound of her own breath, but it's hard when she knows that everyone is gathered underneath, looking at her. She should never have come on this trip, she knows that – and Mum and Dad should have known it too. They said that Nell had a great time at GoCamp, but Tally isn't like Nell. She can't do the things that Nell can do. Right now she doesn't think that she can do *anything* except hold on and try not to shut down.

"You can do it, Tally," says Jade. Her voice is gentle but is carries on the air and Tally hears every word. "You can be brave. Whenever I feel scared I think about how some cats have rescued their kittens from burning buildings and others have protected their owner from bullies. They look at what needs to be done and then they do it. And they do it as fast as they can before they've had time to think about it because sometimes that's the only way to over-come your fears."

"Why are you talking about cats again?" jeers Skye. "Is it because Tally is being a scaredy-cat?"

"Shut up!"

Up on the rock face, Tally blinks. She hasn't heard Jade talk with so much force before.

"Just stop being so horrible," Jade tells Skye. "It's all *your* fault that this is happening in the first place. If you hadn't made so much fuss and gone on about nearly dying when you were perfectly safe the whole time, then Tally wouldn't have any reason to be worried."

"How dare you talk to me like that?" hisses Skye. "If you think that I'm going to let you—"

"Girls!" shouts Kirsten. "That's quite enough!"

"I won't let you fall, Tally!" calls Jade. "Think like a cat and climb!"

Tally hesitates. Cats are brave and so is she because she just stopped herself from having a proper shutdown and that is probably the hardest thing that she's ever done. Slowly, so slowly, she stretches out her fingers and releases her grip on the rock. She reaches up and finds a secure handhold and then she imagines a tiger, coiled and ready to spring. And she pushes with her legs and pulls with her hands and moves up, up, up, and over the top of the cliff.

"You did it!" shouts Jade as Kirsten and Pete start to clap.

Gregory rushes over to where Tally is sitting on the grass.

"Isn't it amazing up here?" he says, not seeming to have any awareness of the drama that has just taken place on the rock face. "Look at the view! I saw a whole school of dolphins a minute ago. And something that looked like a killer whale. No way am I going back out in that water again!"

Tally looks where he's pointing, out across the bay and to the open sea beyond. She isn't convinced about the dolphin part and she can't be bothered to explain to him that killer whales don't eat people, but he's right about the view. And she'd never have seen it if she hadn't persevered.

She stands up and lets the instructor at the top of the cliff unclip the rope from her harness and then she staggers away from the edge and flops back down on to the ground. Her legs are shaking and her heart is racing and she's so tired that she thinks she could probably sleep for a week. But she did it. She didn't give up and that feels so, so good.

"If you think this view is good then you should see this other place that I've found," Gregory says, talking so quickly that his words run together. "It's overlooking the sea and it's really brilliant! I could show you when we've got some free time after lunch. If you want to?"

"No thanks." Tally focuses on the ground and tries to slow her breathing down. "I've got stuff to do."

"Oh." Gregory sounds disappointed but then he shrugs his shoulders and wanders off to see what the instructor is doing.

He's clearly not that bothered about it, which Tally is

glad about. She's got enough problems after her outburst at Skye and Lucy. The last thing she needs is to be seen hanging out with annoying Gregory.

After lunch and the usual hectic canteen, it's free time where everyone gets to choose an activity. Layla tries to convince Tally to go on one of the boat trips with her and the rest of the girls, but Tally has other plans. She overheard Kirsten giving Jade permission to go back to the cabin for some time out, so she can't go there, but she's seen the sign-up sheet on the table and she knows that nobody else has chosen the one thing that she really wants to do, which suits her perfectly. She's been on this trip for more than twenty-four hours now and she needs a break. She needs to go somewhere without any people or noise.

She needs to go to the animal sanctuary.

Tally waits until everyone else has gone and then she makes her way towards the west field. The Sanctuary is in an old barn that has been turned into lots of smaller rooms, and as she approaches, Jack comes out of the main doors, wiping his hands on his trousers.

"Hi!" he calls, spotting her. "Have you come to help out?"

Tally doesn't say a word. She'd forgotten that Jack would be here and she's suddenly regretting coming. She's done with talking and questions and polite smiles and chitchat. All she wants to do is see the animals and let her brain rest for a bit. Her legs start to twitch and her arms start to flap as she gets ready to run.

Jack gives her a closer look and then he turns away and walks back inside the barn, disappearing out of sight. Tally frowns. She was sure he was about to start giving her jobs to do or asking her a thousand questions. She wasn't expecting him to just walk off.

Maybe he thinks that she'll be useless? Maybe he doesn't trust her to look after any of the animals? Maybe—

"This is Frank," says Jack quietly, walking back out through the door. In his hands he is holding a fluffy ball of something that, on closer inspection, turns out to be a guinea pig. "Frank wasn't looked after properly by his owner and he's quite nervous."

He walks across to a bench and waits. He doesn't look at Tally or ask her anything. He just waits.

After a few moments, she moves to the bench and sits down. Jack puts Frank into her arms and she instantly snuggles him close, taking care not to frighten him. His warm body is shaking, and she lowers her head and starts whispering to him, words that nobody else can hear but that Frank seems to understand.

"Hey," she murmurs. "I know that you're nervous because you don't know what's going on. So here's what's going to happen next. I'm going to cuddle you and then I'm going to give you a tasty treat and then I'm going to put some more hay in your bed so that it's all cosy and then I'm going to tuck you up. And tomorrow I'm going to come back and see you for more cuddles and again the day after that and the day after that."

The little animal's body stops shaking and Tally hears the telltale purring sound that guinea pigs make when they are truly relaxed.

"Well, would you listen to that?" whispers Jack. Tally looks up, surprised that he's still there. "I haven't heard Frank make that noise before. He must really like you."

"I like him," Tally says. "Can I keep on holding him for a bit longer?"

Jack nods. "Sure. I've got some jobs to do, so just give me a shout if you need anything. I won't be far away."

And then he goes, leaving Tally and Frank sitting in the warm sunshine. Tally relaxes back against the bench, stroking his fluffy fur and feeling more relaxed than she has done since she left home on Monday morning.

CHAPTER 11

The sun is starting to sink lower in the sky by the time Jack comes to take Frank back to his hutch.

"I told him that I'd give him a treat and some more hay," Tally says, feeling braver after spending so long cuddling the furry guinea pig.

Jack smiles. "You need to head back to the canteen now," he tells her, gently lifting him from her arms. "But I promise that I'll do both those things. Would that be OK?"

Tally nods and stands up. "I guess so."

"Do you like dogs?" Jack pauses at the entrance to the barn and looks back at her. "Because I need someone to take Oscar for a run around in the meadow tomorrow. He's a very daft, very friendly cockapoo whose owners couldn't quite cope with his boisterousness."

Tally grins. "I love dogs," she declares. "I've got a daft

dog of my own at home. He's called Rupert."

"Well, you'll need to bring at least one friend because I can't let you take him on your own," Jack tells her. "But if you haven't got anything else to do then he would love to see you in the afternoon."

He waves one hand and heads into the barn with Frank nestled into the crook of his arm.

Tally turns and starts to walk slowly back to the Centre. There is nothing that she wants to do more tomorrow afternoon than walk Oscar, but what Jack said is going to be a bit of a problem. She doesn't want to invite anyone else to join her at the Sanctuary – the whole point is that she doesn't have to talk to anyone when she's there. But she really does want to meet Oscar the daft cockapoo and so she's going to have to find someone to come with her. The question is – who? Aleksandra is busy with Mina and Tally hasn't even spoken to her since they arrived. Aleksandra does keep trying to wave Tally across to her table, but Tally can see how happy she looks with Mina and the sight of the two of them together makes her red-eyed monster whisper unkind things into her ear. She supposes that she could always ask Layla, but things are still a bit weird between them and she isn't sure that she wants to share this place with her previous best friend.

And that's when it hits her.

She doesn't have a best friend. What she does have is a trail of ex-best friends, all lining up behind her. First Layla and now Aleksandra. Maybe Jade was right. Maybe there's no point in trying to be normal and join in and act like everyone else. Maybe there's no point when all that ever happens is that people disappear, just when she thinks that she can trust them.

Nobody ever stays.

She's probably going to be on her own for ever and ever.

Tally trudges into the canteen where the teachers are handing out pens, paper and envelopes.

"It's the same rules as yesterday," calls Mr Kennedy. "You can choose to stay and write your letter home in here or you can go off and find somewhere quiet. You have thirty minutes and then each envelope needs to be sealed and put in the postbag. Don't forget to write your name on the back of the envelope so that we can check that everyone has added their letter. Off you go!"

Tally grabs her items and then walks straight back outside. There's not enough time to go back to the Sanctuary, but she can't be around everyone else right now. They all seem to find it so easy to be with each other. None of them ever have to worry about whether they're getting it right or if they're saying the wrong thing or moving in the wrong way or generally being different.

She does know another place where she can think and have some peace, though – so as quickly as she can, she heads into the trees and follows the path to the clearing. It might not be as calming as the Sanctuary, but it's quiet and it's peaceful and it's hers.

Except, as she pushes through the bushes, she sees instantly that someone else has found her safe haven.

"Hey!" he yells, dangling off one of the lower branches of the big oak tree that she sat underneath yesterday. "This place is fab, isn't it?"

Gregory drops to the ground and races across to where Tally is standing.

"I mean, it's not as good as the other place that I've found, but it's pretty great! It's like a ready-made den – I reckon I could live here and even if it rained then I wouldn't get wet because the leaves are like a roof, aren't they?" He laughs and spins round with his arms outstretched. "And it's so quiet!"

"It *was*," Tally snaps. "Until you came along."

Gregory stops spinning and looks at her.

"What's wrong with you?" he asks.

It's not a good question to ask Tally, today of all days.

"There is nothing *wrong* with me!" she yells, leaning forward so that her words are directed right at his face. "Just because I don't like being loud all the time and talking constantly and laughing at things that aren't even funny then that doesn't mean that there is something *wrong* with me, OK? Why are you even here? You can go and be with everyone else – this is *my* place."

She pauses to take a deep breath and then glares at him. "Just go away."

Gregory opens his mouth as if he's about to start arguing, but then he seems to change his mind. He gives Tally a sad look, shakes his head and dashes off through the bushes. He's out of sight in seconds, although Tally can hear the sound of him crashing around in the undergrowth for a little while longer until he gets out of earshot and all is quiet again.

But even though it's quiet, it isn't *right*. Tally isn't sure why but the peacefulness of the clearing has gone. She sits down on the fallen branch and tries to write her letter home, but it's even harder than yesterday and she only manage a few lines about what a terrible time she's having before giving up and stuffing it inside the envelope. Then she walks back to the Centre and adds her letter to the postbag, wondering how on earth she is supposed to stay here for another three whole nights.

After supper, the GoCamp instructors organize a quiz night. Tally sits at the table in the canteen and listens while Skye talks loudly about what happened this morning with the rock climbing and how she nearly died but was so incredibly brave. Lucy backs her story and there is no mention of screeching and fuss and drama. Not that Tally cares either way. If Skye wants to pretend that she was brave when she wasn't, then that's her business.

It's dark by the time they all head back to the cabin. The girls are all whispering and sniggering together, and Tally tries to join in with their conversation about which of the boys is the hottest and which is the most annoying, but she doesn't actually care and Lucy and Skye are still giving her the cold shoulder after her outburst at the rock face. It's a relief when Miss Perkins does her rounds and switches off the lights. Even though she isn't at home in her own bed, she thinks that she's so exhausted that she might actually get some sleep tonight.

She closes her eyes and thinks about the things that give her the good feeling.

Rupert.

Being in a car at night listening to the sound of rain on

the roof (or a tent if Mum and Dad are there and they've checked thoroughly for spiders).

Taylor Swift.

The smell the pavements make sometimes after it's rained in summer.

Rupert (again).

Hotel rooms with balconies, especially ones on high-up floors.

Horses quietly munching on hay in their stables with the lovely smell of horse and hay wafting out of the stable door.

Being by the sea (which she actually is right now, so that should be helping).

Home.

If she tries hard enough then she can make her breathing slow and steady. She lets her body sink into the mattress and imagines that she's floating on the waves, letting the water carry her somewhere warm and quiet.

And then Layla gets out of bed and taps her on the leg, ruining all of her efforts.

"Tally!" she whispers loudly. "Come on! It's time!"

Tally raises her head and peers around the dark room. There's a sliver of moonlight coming in through the curtain and she can see Skye, Lucy and Ayesha pulling their clothes on over their pyjamas.

She'd forgotten about the plan to go into the woods tonight.

"I'm not coming," she whispers back to Layla. "I'm all warm and cosy now."

Layla climbs up a few rungs of the ladder so that she's level with Tally's face.

"Oh, please come," she begs. "It'll be way more fun if you're with us. We're meeting up with Khloe's cabin and Skye says that she's got a surprise for us!"

"She doesn't have to come." Skye's voices hisses across the room. "She can stay here with the other loser if she wants to."

Tally glances across to where Jade is curled up on her bed. She is completely still and Tally hopes that she's fast asleep and didn't hear Skye's cruel comment.

"Tally isn't a loser," says Layla, climbing back down the ladder and spinning to face Skye. "That's a horrible thing to say. Take it back!"

"Whatever," drawls Skye, pulling on her trainers. "I didn't say that *she* was a loser, did I?"

"Well, good," snaps Layla. "Because she's our friend and we won't let you talk to her like that, will we?"

The only sound coming from Lucy and Ayesha is that

of Lucy coughing and Ayesha zipping up her jacket.

Tally lowers her head on to her pillow and squeezes her eyes shut. She isn't stupid. This is crunch time, she knows that. If she stays here with Jade then she will spend the rest of the week being on the outside. If she's lucky then maybe Layla will keep on being friendly towards her, but she can't be sure of that. Not when Layla was happy to go along with the rest of them the last time that things went wrong.

But if she gets up and goes with them then the rest of the week could be totally different. She's supposed to be here to experience new things and never in her life has she snuck out into the woods at night. It sounds exciting and scary, and she's terrified of something going wrong, but Mrs Jarman told them that they would all learn to face their fears on this trip and she's not exactly going to do that if she hides in her bed, is she?

Her stomach flips over. Mum and Dad always tell her that she is her own, unique self, and that she doesn't have to be like everyone else – but what do they know about being twelve years old? Maybe, just for once, she wants to do what everyone else is doing.

Not looking at the other bed, Tally sits up and slides down the ladder. Layla gives her a quick hug. Tally quickly pulls a jumper and a pair of baggy tracksuit bottoms over her pyjamas before stuffing her feet into her trainers.

"Let's go then," whispers Skye, tiptoeing towards the door. "Khloe and the rest of her cabin should be there already."

Tally allows Layla to take hold of her hand and then they're outside and running before Miss Perkins or Mr Kennedy can spot them. It's completely dark except for the light reflecting off the moon, and Tally thinks how good it would be to lie down and stare up at the night sky, but Skye has other plans.

"Through here!" she calls, crashing through the bushes and disappearing into the trees. Layla pulls Tally along and they follow Lucy and Ayesha into the wood and down the path. It isn't long until they see lights flickering up ahead and when Layla stops, Tally sees six other girls sitting in a circle around a small campfire.

Her secret clearing is obviously not so secret any more.

"That's genius!" says Skye, striding across and plonking herself next to the girl called Khloe. "Why didn't we think about doing that?"

Khloe laughs. "Because the members of Cabin Six are clearly more intelligent than the members of Cabin One," she teases. She looks across at where Tally is standing with Lucy, Ayesha and Layla. "Are you coming to join us or are you just going to stand there all night?"

Lucy and Ayesha leap forward and join the circle. Layla tugs Tally towards a space and Tally lowers herself to the cold ground. She thinks about the cabin and her warm bed and hopes that this escapade doesn't last too long. Now that she's out here she isn't convinced that *doing what everyone else is doing* is going to be the amazing experience that she was hoping for.

In the middle of the circle, the campfire glows. The girls from Cabin Six have stacked up some leaves and twigs and small flames are licking the air. Tally rubs her hands together and tries not to look at the darkness surrounding them. She usually likes the dark, but here, underneath the trees, it somehow seems menacing and intrusive, like it's pressing in on them. The girls all start talking about a YouTube video where a teenage boy gets lost in the woods and terrifying things start to happen and Tally stares at the campfire, trying to block out their voices. She can do this. She just has to blend in and not start humming or let her arms start flapping the way that they want to, especially if she lets herself think about what would happen if the fire gets out of control and burns GoCamp to the ground.

"So, what's this surprise then?" asks Khloe, after a few minutes. "You said that you had something to show us."

Skye laughs. "Oh, I do." She stands up and pulls something out of her pocket before sitting back down in the circle. "Get ready for the biggest laugh of your lives!"

"What is it?" asks Lucy. "Is that an envelope? Is that one of the letters that we've all been sending home?"

Skye is brandishing a piece of paper in the air and Tally's heart twists. She has no idea what Skye is holding but every bone in her body is telling her that whatever is on that paper is not something that they should be reading.

Skye points at Lucy. "You've got it in one!" she says. "But the question you should be asking is not *is that a letter?* The question you should be asking is *whose letter is it?*"

Khloe's screech of laughter makes Tally jump.

"Oh. My. God. Have you stolen someone's letter? You're terrible, Skye!"

Her voice doesn't sound like she thinks this is terrible in the slightest.

Skye looks at her best friend. "I don't know what you're talking about. I just happened to find this letter lying on the ground earlier and I picked it up for safekeeping. Then

I forgot all about it until just now." Skye glances around the circle. "Do you want me to read it?"

Nine voices shout their approval. Only two stay quiet and next to Tally, Layla squeezes her hand.

"So who wrote it?" asks Lucy. "It'd better not be mine. I wrote a totally lame letter to my mum, telling her that I was having a wonderful time and that GoCamp is the best place ever, but I only said it to make her happy." She sounds anxious and Tally wonders why writing nice things would make her feel worried. "I didn't mean it, obviously. I think this place is rubbish."

"Calm down," Skye tells her, smirking. "I'm sure you wrote a *perfectly adorable* letter home to mummy but you don't need to worry. This wasn't written by you – and I'm pretty sure it's way more pathetic than anything you could possibly come up with."

Lucy nods, looking relieved, as if she doesn't understand that Skye has just insulted her. Tally thinks that it must be nice not to have to second-guess every word that's ever said to you and just take them on face value. She used to be like that too, until she realized that nobody ever says what they mean and you have to work hard to figure out what they're going on about if you don't want to end up making a fool of yourself.

"Anyway," Skye continues. "I'm not going to tell you who wrote it. You have to guess."

Khloe claps her hands and passes her one of the torches.

"Excellent! I love this kind of game. Go for it – read it out!"

Skye clears her throat and starts to read.

"Dear Mum,

"We've only been here for two days but I already know that I'm going to love every single minute of this trip! It's the best thing ever!"

Skye looks up from the page.

"Someone's very enthusiastic, aren't they?"

The girls snigger and Skye lowers her head and keeps reading.

"I'm in a cabin with some wonderful girls and we're all having so much fun! I know that you were a bit anxious about me making friends because year seven has been quite tough so far and my autism hasn't made it any easier, but you really don't need to be worried. I'm hanging out with the nicest girls in the world – in fact, tonight we're going out into the wood for a midnight feast! I can't wait!"

Skye pauses and lets her gaze roam around the group.

"A midnight feast, huh? Are you sure that you didn't

write this, Lucy?"

"No way!" Lucy squeals indignantly. "You know that I didn't."

Skye laughs and Layla leans in towards Tally. "Is this your letter?" she whispers. "Because I'll go and rip it out of her hand right now if it is."

Tally shakes her head. "It's not mine," she whispers back, her stomach starting to swirl. "But we should take it off her anyway. It's not OK to read something that's not addressed to you and this is really personal."

Layla nods but before they can do anything, Skye's voice rings out.

"But the very best part is that I've made a totally new friend! She's funny and popular and clever and so, so pretty and she told me today that she likes me more than anyone else here. And you'll never believe who it is! It's Skye! Yes – the girl who said all those unkind things to me when we started at Redhill High. She said that she didn't mean anything by it and it was all supposed to be a joke, but I just took it all the wrong way. She said that she's going to be my new best friend and we can hang out together every day after school. Isn't that incredible?!"

Skye stops and shakes her head. "Incredible and also deluded. Seriously? As if I would ever say any of that stuff to someone like *her*."

"Who wrote the letter?" pleads Khloe. "Come on – you have to tell us!"

"You need to stop reading this," says Tally, getting to her feet. "It's private and we shouldn't be doing this."

"Ooh, get you!" crows Skye, also standing up. "You should just be thankful that it wasn't *your* tragic letter that I found."

Tally's eyes narrow and she takes a step forward.

"Give it to me," she demands.

"Make me," snarls Skye, dancing out of reach and shining the torch on to the paper.

"She says that she likes the way I stood up to her when we were climbing today and that nobody ever speaks to her like that. And all it took to make a difference was me being a bit braver, like you're always telling me to be! She loves cats almost as much as I do and I can't wait to introduce her to Mr Tibbles – after all, he's the cutest cat in the universe."

Tally's head starts to buzz. She knows exactly who wrote this letter and Skye has gone too far. She lunges forward with her hands outstretched, just as there's a cry from the trees behind them.

"Stop it! Just stop it!"

Tally freezes as every head turns towards the voice.

She watches as Jade staggers out into the clearing. The moonlight trickling through the leaves makes her face look pale. Her hands are shaking.

"How have you got that?" she cries, pointing at the letter in Skye's hand. "Did you steal it from the postbag?"

"Of course it's *her* letter!" says Khloe, snorting back a laugh. "Who else would be so pathetic as to make up a fictitious friendship and lie to their mum?"

"I wasn't lying to her!" shouts Jade. "Skye said all of those things to me." Her eyes open wide as she stares at the other girl. "You told me that we could be friends and you told me to come and join you out here once you'd all left the cabin. You know you did!"

Skye takes a step forward and drops the letter on the floor, before starting to clap very slowly.

"And you fell for every word that I said, didn't you? Honestly – you're so easy to trick that it's hardly even fun. You're crazy."

Jade wraps her arms around her stomach, as if she's about to be sick.

"You were lying?" she whispers. "When you said that you wanted to be my friend?"

Skye walks across to where Khloe is sitting and drops down next to her, slinging her arm around Khloe's shoulder.

"You figure it out, Kitty. I did say one thing that was true though." She stares up at Jade, her eyes suddenly hard. "Nobody speaks to me like that."

Jade wails and spins around, racing out of the clearing and into the dark night.

And Tally, whose feet have been frozen to the ground throughout this entire conversation, suddenly becomes unstuck.

"You are a horrible human being," she says, marching up to Skye and bending down so that their noses are almost touching. "You are mean and selfish and you're a bully and you don't deserve to have any friends, definitely not someone as nice as Jade."

She glares at Skye and then swoops across to where the letter is lying on the ground. "I thought that being part of your group would make this week better but I was wrong. I'd rather spend the rest of the week on my own than be with anyone who thinks that what just happened is OK."

"That's a good job!" yells Skye as Tally storms across the clearing. "Because alone is what you're going to be when I tell everyone how much of a loser you are! You're going to regret this, Tally!"

Tally ignores her and pushes her way through the bushes, intent on catching up with Jade. She knows that she has just slammed a huge door shut in her own face and that the rest of the week is going to be unbearable, but there's no way that she could sit by and watch someone be treated so badly.

"Jade!" she calls, seeing her up ahead. "Wait for me!"

"Just leave me alone!" The words bounce off the trees, dripping with hurt. "You're as bad as they are for letting them treat me like this! Just go away!"

Jade breaks into a sprint and Tally skids to a halt, letting her go. She was only trying to help. Jade didn't have to be so rude to her and it's not as if Tally is the same as Skye and the others, is it? Jade shouldn't go around yelling at innocent people who haven't even done anything in the first place.

An uneasy thought creeps into Tally's head and she leans against a tree. Maybe that's the problem? Maybe Jade is right and she should have done something. There have been a thousand opportunities to step in and do something. In the cabin. During the raft building. When they were at the rock climbing. Someone should have stopped Skye behaving so badly and that someone could have been Tally.

She was so busy trying not to be on the *outside* that she forgot to wonder whether she really wanted to be part of their *inside*.

"Tally!" Layla comes crashing through the trees. "Wait for me! Skye's wrong – you're not on your own and you're not a loser. What you said back there was really brave – I wish that I could be as courageous as you are."

She gives Tally a hug and, for the first time in a long time, Tally feels like her old friend is properly with her.

"You're here, aren't you?" she tells her, hugging her back. "That's quite brave. And I'm not brave – if I was then I'd have stopped Skye when she first started being so awful."

"Where's Jade?" asks Layla, looking around. "We need to find her and make this OK."

Tally shakes her head. "I don't think we can. She hates us as much as she hates Skye and the others. It's too late."

The two girls walk slowly back to the cabin, only picking up speed when they dash from the trees to the building, desperately hoping that all the teachers are safely inside their own rooms. Inside Cabin One, it is dark and quiet and the only evidence that Jade is back is a curled-up shape under her duvet. Tally doesn't want to disturb her, so she writes in her journal using her torch for light and then puts the letter carefully inside the cover so she can return it to Jade in the morning.

And then she lies awake until the three other girls sneak back in, the frosty air that fills the cabin on their return coming from more than just the open door and the chilly night breeze.

Date: Tuesday 16th June.

Situation: Second day of camp.

Anxiety rating: 6. Discovering the Sanctuary has helped me to feel calmer.

Dear Diary,

What a long, long day it's been.

Good things that happened today:

Only one, really – I got to hang out with Frank the guinea pig. He was really soft and had funny long hair. Holding him makes me feel very safe and relaxed almost like I'm in heaven.

Bad things that happened today (in order of badness):

Annoying Gregory invaded my safe space. From now on I shall think of him as the space invader.

I got stuck up on a rock face hundreds of feet high in the sky. All because awful Skye panicked me. I almost went into shutdown. Shutdown is totally different from meltdown, but in a way is even scarier. In meltdown I have no choice but to blow – it's like the top of my head comes off and everything comes out: shouting, insults, screaming, crying, hitting, kicking, rocking, whatever. In shutdown I have no choice but to freeze. I can't move or talk and it feels like I can't even blink. People think I'm doing it on purpose, but there is absolutely no choice. It doesn't happen to me very often but when it does it is just as exhausting as a meltdown. It's almost as though I am not there. Although it's very different to a meltdown, I need just the same things to help me. Someone calm and kind, with a soft voice, and a very light touch, and absolutely no demands or commands whatsoever.

But the biggest bad thing of all was how mean Skye was tonight. She excelled herself in the vileness stakes. She read out Jade's very private letter, which was just despicable. And what makes it even worse is that now we all know that Jade is autistic and she might not have wanted us to have that information. Her autism, her choice to tell or not. And that choice has been taken away in such a nasty way. I tried to stand up for her but just shattered when Skye looked at me. I wish I'd tried harder. Now I know how Layla felt last term when she didn't stand up for me. I get it now.

CHAPTER 12

The atmosphere in Cabin One is subdued when the girls wake up the next morning. Tally gets dressed as quickly as she can and walks across to where Jade is pulling on her shoes.

"Do you want to sit with Layla and me at breakfast time?" she asks but Jade doesn't even look up, and after a few more attempts to engage her in conversation, Tally leaves her alone. She doesn't blame her for refusing to talk.

The bell rings for breakfast and Jade races out of the cabin, disappearing before the rest of them have even managed to get through the door.

"She hates us," Tally says to Layla. "We should have done something to help her before and now it's too late."

"Oh, give it a rest," says Skye, coming up behind them.

"She'll get over it."

Tally glares at her and Skye laughs before sauntering off towards the canteen.

"She's really unkind," says Layla, as Lucy and Ayesha join them. "Do you think we should tell Mr Kennedy about Skye taking Jade's letter?"

"No way!" exclaims Lucy. "It was only a joke and it's not OK to snitch. It's not Skye's fault that Jade hasn't got a sense of humour."

Tally turns to look at her. "It wasn't a joke," she says slowly. "Jokes are funny. Taking Jade's private letter and reading it out to everyone wasn't even a little bit funny."

Lucy shakes her head. "Look – Skye might have gone a bit far, but she didn't mean anything by it. I'll tell her to say sorry to Jade and then we can forget all about it."

But Tally isn't daft. She knows Skye absolutely *did* mean something by it. She meant to hurt and embarrass Jade. An apology isn't going to take that away and it certainly isn't going to make Jade *forget* about it.

"Skye isn't going to stop being mean to Jade," she tells Lucy. "And she isn't sorry so there's no point in trying to make her apologize unless she really means it."

Layla nods. "We need to find Jade and make it better," she says, stepping closer to Tally. "We can all hang out together – we don't need Skye and her friends to make this week fun. I bet she's gone down to the beach – we can go and find her now before breakfast."

Lucy and Ayesha look at each other and there's a moment of silence. Tally sees their eyes dart between the Centre and the path towards the beach as if they're trying to make a decision.

"Skye's not that bad," says Lucy eventually, shuffling her feet on the ground. "She's a laugh and she's got loads of friends at Redhill High."

"Yeah," adds Ayesha. "I mean, I totally agree that reading Jade's letter was a bit out of order, but she's really fun to hang out with and I'm sure she was only messing with Jade – she didn't mean to upset her."

Tally stands up as tall as she possibly can.

"Is that what you were doing when you stole my tiger mask and gave it to Luke?" she asks. Her voice is quiet – but it's the kind of quiet that happens just before thunder cracks open the sky. "Were you just *messing* with me?"

Lucy's mouth drops open in surprise. The incident with the mask and Luke and telling everyone about Tally's autism hasn't been spoken about since it happened, almost as if they'd all agreed that it was something that had magically disappeared.

"Because I know that you all thought it was just a joke," Tally continues, staring at Lucy. "But it hurt me and it was really hard to come back to school after it happened. So really, as jokes go, it was pretty much an abject failure."

"I didn't think it was a joke." Layla's voice is quiet and when Tally looks at her, she can see that her friend's cheeks are flushed with a deep red colour. "And what Skye did taking Jade's letter wasn't a joke either. That's why we need to find her. We need to let her know that we don't think it's OK."

Ayesha glances at Lucy. "We didn't mean to hurt you," she tells Tally. "And we're sorry, we really are. But we like Skye and we don't want to stop being friends with her."

Lucy nods. "Jade isn't one of us," she says. "I'm not trying to be mean, but she just isn't."

Tally thinks for a second and then nods as she realizes what she's been getting wrong.

"You're right," she says. "And I'm not one of you either. We're totally different but it's OK."

"What do you mean?" Lucy sounds confused.

Tally looks at her. "You should totally go and hang out with Skye," she tells her. "You like her and she's your friend so it's all good. Jade told me that people like us would always be on the outside and people like you would always be on the inside, but she was wrong. There isn't an inside and an outside – it's just about being with the people who *know* you."

"So you aren't going to be angry if we stay friends with Skye?" asks Ayesha. "Because you're our friend too, Tally."

"You can be friends with whoever you want," Tally says, shrugging. "And so can I."

She smiles at Layla, who beams back at her.

"*I* know you," Layla tells her. "Does that mean that we're proper friends again?"

Tally laughs. "Yes," she says. "We're proper friends and I think I know you too."

Then she links her arm with Layla's before turning and striding towards the beach, intent on finding Jade and making things right.

"I really am sorry about what happened when we started year seven," Layla says, as they head down the path. "I've missed having you as my friend. I've been kind of lonely without you."

"Me too," Tally agrees. "And that's how I know that we have to find Jade. It's awful being all on your own, with nobody caring how you feel."

But when they step out on to the sand, the beach is empty and there is no sign that anybody has been down here this morning.

"Perhaps she went straight in for breakfast?" suggests Layla. "Let's go up to the canteen and see if she's there."

They can hear the noise coming from the Centre before they even step inside. The canteen is filled with kids yelling at each other and racing around the room, and when Tally steps through the door, the sounds threaten to drown her.

"Where are the teachers?" she asks, scrunching up her face. "This is awful."

"I don't know!" Layla shouts back. "But I can see Jade sitting over there." She points towards a table on the far side of the room. They start to make their way across the heaving hall, but they haven't even got halfway before a loud bellowing voice makes everyone freeze.

"Settle down!" booms Mr Kennedy. "Anyone not in a seat in the next ten seconds will be on toilet-cleaning duty for the rest of today and tomorrow!"

Layla pulls Tally down into the nearest empty chair and they stare as the teachers and all the staff from GoCamp troop into the room, their faces sombre.

"Everybody pay attention!" shouts Mr Kennedy. "We have a very serious situation and you all need to listen."

Tally twists her head to look at Layla. "What's going

on?" she whispers. "What's he on about?"

Layla shrugs her shoulders.

"I don't know," she whispers back. "But it sounds bad."

"Yesterday, some of the letters that have been written by students went missing," Mr Kennedy continues. "If it was just one or two then we probably would have thought that they'd merely been misplaced, but there are at least twenty letters missing and that's no accident. So – if anyone knows anything about this then they need to speak up now."

The canteen descends into a heavy silence. Kids glance at each other and there are a lot of worried faces, but nobody says a word. Tally's heart starts thudding in her chest. She knows who took at least one of the letters – but knowing and telling are two very different things. Next to her, Layla reaches out and squeezes her hand. Tally isn't sure what she's trying to say, but she clamps her lips tightly together and stares at the floor. The last time she told a teacher when someone had done something wrong it all went very badly, and she ended up losing all her friends. Not that the *telling* was necessarily the reason why she ended up alone but everything started from that – and she's reluctant to repeat the experience.

"Well, I can't say that I'm surprised but I *am* disappointed," says Mr Kennedy, when it becomes obvious that nobody is going to speak. "In that case, you leave us with no choice. We're going to have to search every cabin and tent until we find the letters."

The room erupts.

"You can't do that!" yells a boy from Redhill High. "It's a violation of our privacy!"

"Settle down!" hollers Mr Limpkin. "And I think you'll find that taking other people's letters is a *violation of privacy*."

"I think it's a good idea," calls Skye from a table near the back of the room. "I just hope that nobody has taken *my* letter and read it." She shudders. "The idea of someone reading my personal thoughts is horrifying."

"There's no need to get upset," says Mr Limpkin. "We're going to find the perpetrator and they will be dealt with accordingly."

The teachers leave the canteen with several of the GoCamp staff, and the room fills once again with noise.

"I bet it was Gregory!" yells Khloe. "He's always getting into trouble."

"Shut up!" screeches Gregory. "I'd never do anything like that."

"Yeah, Khloe – don't be unkind," says Skye, her clear

voice floating across the canteen. "We all know Gregory can't read, so why would he have stolen the letters?"

Gregory screws up his face as people start to laugh, and Tally leans closer to Layla.

"If they search our cabin then they're going to find wherever Skye put the letters," she whispers. "So why is Skye so happy?"

Layla frowns. "There's no way that she's left them in the cabin," she tells Tally. "She must have hidden them somewhere else. Or maybe she destroyed them last night after we left."

The minutes tick by and Tally starts to feel more and more uneasy, as if there's a snake pit in her stomach. She should speak up and tell someone what Skye has done. There are rules about how people need to behave, and Tally knows what happens when the rules aren't followed. Everything goes so wrong that sometimes it can't be made right, no matter how hard you try.

But she can also hear Nell's voice in her head, telling her to mind her own business and asking her why she always ends up putting herself in the middle of trouble. Maybe she *can't* make this better. Maybe she just has to let it go and move on.

It isn't long before the teachers step back into the

canteen and the room goes quiet.

"Can everyone from Cabin One please step outside?" says Mr Kennedy, his voice low. "The rest of you can chat amongst yourselves for a few minutes."

"Oooooh!" The jeers rise up and spread around the room and Tally feels her heart starting to race again.

"I knew it!" squeals Skye, holding her hands up to her mouth. "My letter was taken, wasn't it? Oh – it's like they've read my diary or something!"

Khloe puts her arm around Skye's shoulder and pulls her in for a hug.

"Don't worry," she says, her voice loud. "They're going to get what they deserve for being so sneaky."

"It's OK, Skye," call several voices from around the room. "It'll all be OK!"

Skye sniffs theatrically and Tally wonders how anyone can possibly be falling for her act.

"Cabin One outside, please!" repeats Mr Kennedy. "Now."

Tally and Layla stand up and walk towards the door, with Lucy, Ayesha and Skye close behind them. As they reach the exit, Tally sees Jade making her way towards them. Her face is pale and she looks like she's about to cry.

"We have a problem," says Mr Kennedy, as soon as

they are standing outside on the verandah. Mr Limpkin, the teacher from Redhill High, walks over to join them along with Miss Perkins, who puts her hands on her hips and glares at Tally. Tally feels her legs starting to wobble. They know what Skye did and they're going to ask why she didn't tell them sooner.

"We have found one of the missing letters," continues Mr Kennedy. "And it was in your cabin."

Tally opens her mouth but he carries on before she can speak.

"I know that being away from home can be challenging," he says. "But I'm really very shocked that a pupil from Kingswood Academy could behave like this."

Kingswood Academy?

Tally turns to look at Layla, who looks just as confused as she feels.

"But it wasn't—" she starts before Mr Kennedy puts his hand up and stops her.

"This isn't the time for more lies and excuses," he snaps. "Tally – I am extremely disappointed in this behaviour from you. I'm going to have to phone your parents and we'll discuss what needs to be done."

Tally stares at him, trying to understand what he's saying. She knows that she should have spoken up about Skye, but surely he doesn't need to phone her mum and dad?

"We just can't understand why you'd do this," adds Miss Perkins. "It seems completely out of character."

"I didn't want to get in trouble," Tally says, glancing at Skye. "I know that I should have told you last night."

"Honesty would certainly have helped, but it still doesn't change what you did," says Mr Kennedy, sighing deeply. "And despite the fact that we know you have your own challenges, we can't ignore the fact that you stole something that doesn't belong to you."

An icy trickle of fear drips down Tally's spine and she blinks hard, trying to make sense of his words.

"I haven't stolen anything," she stumbles. "I wouldn't."

"The letter was in *your* journal, Tally." Miss Perkins fixes her with a hard look. "Which was underneath your pillow. How do you explain that if you didn't take it?"

"Did you read my journal?" The words burst out of Tally's mouth like tiny explosions. "That's my personal diary. You had no right to look at it."

"That's hardly the point here," barks Miss Perkins. "You aren't exactly in a position to be complaining about your rights when you took someone else's letter."

"I didn't take anything," shouts Tally. "I just put Jade's

letter there to keep it safe until I could give it to her."

"So are you saying that you just *found* her letter?" asks Mr Kennedy, frowning. "I'm sure you can appreciate that this sounds incredibly far-fetched. It would be much better if you just told the truth."

"She's such a liar," adds Skye. "I bet she's got all the other letters too."

"No! You don't understand," starts Layla, stepping forward. "Tally would never—"

"Let Tally speak for herself, please," interrupts Miss Perkins.

But Tally cannot speak any more. The fury and the fear and the absolute unfairness of the whole situation have stolen her words. Her hands start to flap and her legs start to shake and the people standing in front of her fade into a blur. She closes her eyes and clenches her fists, and even though she always works so hard not to let a meltdown happen when she's away from home, she opens her mouth, ready to scream and shout and do whatever it takes to make them see the truth.

"It was Skye."

The words are so quiet that they take a moment to push their way through the angry hissing in Tally's ears and even then, she can't be sure that she's heard them properly.

"It was Skye. She took the letters. Tally didn't do anything."

Tally opens her eyes and looks in the direction of the voice. Jade is jiggling from one foot to the other, her face bright red and her eyes shining with tears, but even though she's clearly afraid, her words are clear.

"That's a lie!" screeches Skye. "She's just trying to protect Tally!"

"It's not a lie," says Layla, grabbing Tally's hand. "Tally would never steal anything. She was trying to give the letter *back* to Jade, not take it from her."

"She's lying too!" shouts Skye, looking at Mr Limpkin. "It's their word against ours." She glances at Lucy and Ayesha, who are standing next to her, and then back at the teacher. "You're not going to listen to *them*, are you? Not when the three of us can tell you exactly what happened?"

"It does make it rather difficult," says Mr Limpkin, turning towards Mr Kennedy and Miss Perkins. "If they're all going to be telling a completely different story."

There's a second of pause and then Layla speaks up.

"Skye had Jade's letter last night so she must have taken it from the postbag. We all saw her." She looks at Lucy and Ayesha, who are standing next to Skye. "Didn't we?"

The look of panic that floods across both their faces is almost funny. Almost. Tally watches the two girls stare at each other, having an entire conversation without saying a single word. Their eyes dart between Tally and Layla and then move on to Skye, and Tally's heart feels like it misses a beat. There's no way that these girls will defend her. She's been here before and she knows how this story ends.

"I didn't want to say anything before because I didn't want to get anyone in trouble," says Skye, her voice suddenly soft and gasping, a bit like a baby. "But last night, Tally showed us all Jade's letter. She read it out loud to everyone and said some really unkind things."

The world goes red, right in front of Tally's eyes.

"I DID NOT!" she bellows, stepping towards Skye. "You're a liar!"

"Girls!" Mr Kennedy moves into Tally's path. "This behaviour is unacceptable! Somebody in Cabin One took the letter and I intend to get to the bottom of it."

"It was Tally!" insists Skye. "You know it was! Maybe she didn't mean to do it – maybe she didn't even know that it was wrong, but it was definitely her."

The rage that floods Tally's body is so strong that, for a brief moment, it seems to her that the world stops turning.

"It *was* Skye." Lucy's voice is shaky but loud enough

225

for everyone to hear and the world starts to rotate once more. "She was the one who took Jade's letter and shared it with us all."

Ayesha nods. "Tally only had it because she wanted to give it back to Jade."

Skye narrows her eyes and glares at the girls, who both take a step away from her. "They're just saying that because they're all from the same school," she whines. "This is *so* unfair."

Mr Limpkin nods. "It does seem rather difficult to prove anything," he says to Mr Kennedy and Miss Perkins. "Especially when the evidence was found in a bed belonging to a pupil from *your* school."

"Skye has got the rest of the letters inside her swim bag," says Jade. "I saw her hiding them in there this morning. Then she put the bag under her mattress."

Skye twists her head to look at Jade. "No you didn't!" she exclaims. "That's another lie. There was nobody in the cabin when I did that because I—"

She trails off and Mr Kennedy raises an eyebrow at Mr Limpkin.

"Would you like to take it from here?"

Mr Limpkin scowls. "I'll deal with this." He points at Skye. "You, young lady, are in some serious trouble.

You can expect a rather difficult conversation with your parents in the very near future."

Skye bursts into tears and Mr Limpkin gestures towards the door, waiting until she's gone ahead before following her, his face grim.

"I'm very sorry about all that, Tally," says Mr Kennedy, turning back to the girls. "That was a very difficult situation to deal with."

"It's fortunate that you've got some good friends to speak up for you," adds Miss Perkins. "That's the kind of team spirit that I like to see from Kingswood Academy pupils."

Layla glares at her. "You thought that Tally was a liar," she states. "So where's your team spirit?"

Miss Perkins puts her hands on her hips and narrows her eyes. "Watch your attitude," she warns Layla. "Any more of that and you'll be the one being sent home."

Mr Kennedy walks across to where Tally is standing and leans down so that only she can hear him. "Do you want to go home?" he asks gently. "I completely understand if you do, and I'll explain everything to your parents. I know that you've not had the easiest time so far, and I'm sorry that we haven't acted sooner to make things better. I've had your friend Aleksandra on at me about five times a day, requesting that we let you share their tent, but you seemed to be fine in Cabin One." He pauses, his face wrinkling in a frown. "We should have checked in on you."

"I did tell you," Tally reminds him. "I told you when we first got here."

Mr Kennedy nods. "I know. And I'm really sorry. So do you want to go home?"

Tally hesitates. All she's wanted to do since she got here is to leave. But things feel a little different now. She doesn't feel quite so alone. And OK, it took her nearly getting into serious trouble to make Lucy and Ayesha stand up for her, but they still actually did it. And she's got Layla, who is possibly the fiercest friend ever, plus someone needs to walk Oscar the excitable cockapoo this afternoon, and maybe Jade doesn't think that she's an entirely horrible person after all. And it turns out that Aleksandra hasn't forgotten about her after all. Maybe she was a bit quick to assume that her friend had just abandoned her for someone else?

"I'll stay," she tells him. He nods and then beckons to Miss Perkins.

"You girls can have some time to yourselves," he tells them. "There's plenty to explore in the grounds and you need to make sure you're back here for lunch but otherwise, a bit of free time might be a good thing."

The teachers disappear inside the canteen and the five girls look at each other.

"Sorry about all that," mutters Lucy. "We shouldn't have let it get so far."

Ayesha links her arm with Lucy's. "We thought she was exciting to be around," she says to Tally. "But we couldn't let you get the blame for something that she did."

"How did you know that Skye had the letters in her swim bag?" Layla asks Jade. "She said that there was nobody else in the cabin."

Jade gives a small smile. "I'm invisible to them, aren't I?" She waves her hands, taking in the canteen and the retreating backs of Lucy and Ayesha. "I was lying on my bed, but she didn't think to check there because she doesn't ever see me. Even when I'm right in front of her. I can't believe that I was stupid enough to think that she'd ever want to be friends with me."

"We can see you," Tally tells her, holding out her arm. "And we'd like to be friends with you. If you want to be our friend, that is. I know we're not exactly the same, but I know what it's like to find things extra-hard. I'm autistic too."

Jade blinks and then nods her head. "I'd like that," she

says quietly, linking arms with Tally. "I'd like that a lot."

"So it's official then," Tally declares. "We are friends and nobody should even think about messing with us because we might be small but we are fierce."

She grabs Layla's hand and, still holding on to Jade, starts to march off towards the west field, in the direction of the Sanctuary. "Also, do you like dogs? Because I know a cockapoo called Oscar who needs walking."

CHAPTER 13

At lunchtime, the canteen is filled with chatter about the letters and what happened. Tally walks inside and stops as soon as the first questions fly through the air towards her.

"What happened?" calls Ameet. "We heard that you got the blame for the letters but that it was someone else who took them."

"It was Skye!" yells another boy. "I heard that she threatened to burn down the cabin if any of them told on her!"

"I heard that she pushed Tally into the bay and left her there to drown!" shouts a girl from across the room.

"I'm standing *right here*," she murmurs to Layla and Jade. "*And* I can swim. What are they on about?"

"It's the drama," Jade tells her, looking around the room. "Nothing is ever actually dramatic enough so they have to make it sound more than it really is."

Luke stands up and slams his hand on the table, getting everyone's attention. "If anyone else from Redhill High thinks that they can have a go at Tally then they'd better be prepared to deal with me," he growls. Then he looks across at where Tally is standing and nods his head sharply.

"All right?" he says gruffly.

Tally has no idea why he is suddenly so interested in her wellbeing, but this doesn't feel like the right time to ask him, so she does what she always does when people start acting bizarrely and copies him.

"All right," she barks back, giving a quick nod.

It works and he sits down, seemingly satisfied with her response.

"I heard that Skye is on toilet-cleaning duty until we leave!" calls someone.

"I heard that she's being excluded from school!" shouts another. "She's going to have to be home-educated."

"I can't stay in here," mutters Tally to Layla. "It's too much."

"Hang on." Layla strides across the room to where Mr Kennedy has just entered through the side door. She talks to him for a moment, pointing to where Tally and Jade are standing, and then he nods.

"We're allowed to fill our plates and then take our food outside," she tells them, coming back across the crowded canteen. "He said that as long as we stay on the verandah outside then it's fine for us to eat every meal out there for the rest of the week."

She hands them each a plate and, as quickly as they can, they choose some food and then make their escape. Outside, the sun is shining and the noise of the canteen and the endless questions about Skye and the letters fade into the distance. The girls make their way towards one of the picnic tables and settle themselves down.

"This sandwich is not the best sandwich I have ever tasted," says Tally, taking a tiny nibble of her cheese sandwich. "But I've eaten all the snack bars that Mum packed in my bag and I am so hungry."

Jade nods. "Tell me about it. It's the wrong bread *and* the wrong cheese. I've got some flapjacks back at the cabin though and you can have one later if you like? My mum sent me with way too much food."

"Thanks," says Tally. "That'd be great."

She breathes out deeply and smiles at the other girl. She's never had an autistic friend before and it feels really, really good. Like she isn't quite as different as she thought she was.

"I can't wait to go back to the Sanctuary later," says Jade, grinning back. "This morning was amazing! Oscar is gorgeous but I'm most excited about seeing the hens. Jack said that there are some baby chicks who have just hatched and that I can hold them if I'm really careful."

Tally smiles at her. "Maybe we can figure out a way of not having to do any more of the activities and just spend the rest of the time there," she says. "I don't mind being here if we can just be us and the animals."

"There's no way that they'll let us do that," says Layla, opening a packet of crisps and offering them around. "Apparently we all have to participate in every single task."

Suddenly, the door to the canteen flies open and noise pours out on to the verandah. Tally's heart sinks as she sees Gregory, the noisiest boy that she has ever met, race across and throw himself on to the bench opposite her.

"Mr Limpkin has sent me outside to eat, which isn't very kind, is it?" he says, the words bursting from his mouth. "He says that I'm too much of a disruption to be with everyone else, which is really unfair because I was only asking a question about when the ham in the ham sandwiches goes out of date because I thought it smelt a little bit funny, and ham does smell funny when it's gone bad, doesn't it? And I don't want to get food poisoning so it was a fair question to ask, don't you think?"

The girls gape at him, trying to figure out what the question actually is.

"Anyway, I'm not going to eat it, just in case," he continues, picking up an apple and taking a huge bite. "Hey – that tree is a bit close to the building, isn't it?" He points at a tree across the clearing. "If there's a storm and it gets hit by lightning then it could easily fall on top if us and we'd all be killed." He looks anxiously at the sky. "Does anybody know what the weather forecast is?"

Tally leans back her head and gazes up at the bright blue sky that doesn't have even a single cloud in sight.

"I'm pretty sure that there are no storms forecast," she tells him.

Gregory nods, looking relieved. "That's good." He finishes his apple and then looks around the table, seeming to see the three girls properly for the first time.

"Hey – you go to my school, don't you?" He stares at Jade and her cheeks start to flush. "You're that Cat Girl."

"Don't you ever—" snaps Tally, but Gregory is still talking.

"Yeah! It *is* you! You know everything in the world about cats and you're always talking about them and it's all because of you that I've even got a cat, so I should probably say thank you to you because if I hadn't told my dad all that stuff that I heard you saying about cats being excellent at lowering stress levels and having a calming effect on people then he'd never have agreed to let me have Hulk."

He pauses and takes a deep breath. "Thank you."

"Have you had Hulk for long?" asks Tally, frowning. "Because I'm not sure that he's doing a very good job of calming you down."

Beside her, Layla makes a spluttering sound that starts off as a laugh but turns into a cough.

Gregory looks confused. "I've had him for six months and I'm super-calm now. Or at least, I am when I'm at home with Hulk."

"Cats *are* brilliant," Jade agrees, grinning at Layla. "I'm glad that your dad let you get one."

Gregory smiles at her. "Well, if I hadn't heard you talking about all that stuff then I'd never have been able to persuade him. You're a brilliant Cat Girl!"

"Don't call her that," Tally tells him. "It's not nice to call people names."

"Oh." Gregory's face falls. "I didn't mean—"

"It's fine," says Jade, her words tumbling out as if they're in a hurry to be heard. "I don't mind."She turns to

Tally. "It's not the same when he says it," she tells her. "He isn't saying it because he thinks it's a bad thing. It isn't the *name* that makes me feel sad – it's what they mean when they say it."

"I really *don't* think it's bad," adds Gregory, blinking quickly. "I think being Cat Girl is cool. It makes you sound like a superhero and having a nickname is brilliant."

Jade nods. "I think it sounds cool too," she tells him.

Tally tilts her head to one side and looks at him. "You know something?" she says slowly. "You should really be called Gory. You're always going on about scary accidents and it's a way better name for you."

Layla grins. "It's perfect," she agrees.

"It sounds a bit like a superhero too," Jade laughs. "Maybe a superhero who can deal with any emergency and never panics!"

Gory looks at them, as if he's checking to see if they're teasing him or not.

"Only if you like it though," says Tally quickly. "We'll keep calling you Gregory if you'd rather."

"I like it," he tells her. "I've always wanted a nickname but nobody has ever liked me enough to give me one."

"Gory it is, then," says Jade.

"Hey – do you want to see something brilliant?" he asks

them, his eyes shining with excitement. "I've found this really great place and I could show you?"

"I think we've already got plans," says Layla, and then the door to the canteen opens again and people start to walk through, pushing and shoving each other in an attempt to leave first. Gory lowers his head and when Tally looks over at him, she can see his fingers drumming on the top of the table. She isn't sure that she's ever seen him actually be still, even for a second.

"Hey! Gregory! Have you been sent outside to the reject table?" yells a boy from Redhill High, making the people around him start to laugh. "Are you sure that it's safe out here? I'd hate for you to get attacked by a ham sandwich."

"I didn't say that it was going to attack me," murmurs Gregory, his head sinking lower. "And they'll be sorry if they all get food poisoning."

"We're all going down to the bay," calls the boy. "Just so you know where *not* to go, OK?"

And then they move on, jostling each other and trying to trip each other up while their sharp, barbed words fly through the air and hit their target.

Gory waits until they've gone and then stands up.

"See you," he mutters. "I guess I'll go and find somewhere else to be."

Tally looks at Jade and then at Layla, her eyes raised in a silent question. Both girls nod back at her.

"I bet you're missing Hulk," Tally says, jumping to her feet. "I'm missing my dog. He's called Rupert and he's only got three legs but he's the bravest and best dog in the universe."

"I'm missing Mr Tibbles," says Jade. "I'd say that he is the best cat in the universe but Hulk sounds pretty good too, so maybe they're both the best."

Layla skips towards the steps. "We're going to the Sanctuary and I don't know if there are any cats there, but Jack has got guinea pigs and chickens and a dog called Oscar."

Gory swallows. "It sounds nice," he says quietly.

Tally turns around and walks across to where Layla is standing, with Jade close behind her. "I can't wait to see Oscar again. Jack said that I can groom him this afternoon!"

The three girls leap down on to the ground and start to walk towards Sanctuary. After a few steps, Tally pauses and turns. Gory is still standing on the verandah.

"Aren't you coming with us then?"

Gory whoops and launches himself off the verandah.

"Yes!" he shouts. "I want to see the animals! Let's go!"

And then he races on ahead, pausing every few moments to yell at them to speed up.

"He's going to have to calm down if he wants to cuddle the guinea pigs," observes Tally as they follow him down the path. "He'll scare them to death if he keeps behaving like that."

"He'll be calm," Layla assures her. "Just wait and see. Jack will sort him out."

By the time the girls reach the Sanctuary, Gory has already arrived and is crouched on the floor next to Jack.

"Hey!" calls Tally, and Gory spins round, his finger shoved against his lips.

"Don't be so loud!" he whispers. At least, Tally thinks that it's supposed to be a whisper. They can probably hear him down by the bay.

The girls tiptoe up to where Jack is pulling something out of a wooden run and handing it to Gory.

"He was brought in last night," Jack tells them. "Someone found him abandoned by the side of the road."

Tally stares at the tiny kitten fast asleep in Gory's arms.

"Why would anybody leave him?" she asks. "That's horrible."

Jack shakes his head. "People abandon animals for all kinds of reasons," he says. "Maybe they can't afford to feed them or they think that the animal is badly behaved. Or sometimes, the animal might have something wrong with it and the owner doesn't want to keep it."

"You can't just give up on something because it isn't perfect," mutters Gory. "You have to keep on loving it and help it to be the best that it can be."

Tally doesn't know why but she suddenly wants to cry.

"Well, you sound like you're exactly the kind of person who should be helping out here," Jack tells Gory.

"Yeah," agrees Layla. "We're lucky that you came to join us."

"Join you?" Gory tears his eyes away from the kitten. "What do you mean?"

"You can hang out with us," Layla explains. "If you want to."

"Everyone is welcome," says Jade, and Tally stares at her in surprise, running the words through her head.

Everyone is welcome? Is that really how this is going to work? If everyone is welcome then surely that takes away the specialness of the group?

Tally turns away and walks across to the fence by the meadow where Oscar the dog is racing around, chasing his own tail. She's been friends with Layla for ever and it was her choice to invite Jade into the group. If they're going to start bringing other people in then it's not going to be the same. It's not going to feel safe. She doesn't even know Gory, so how is she supposed to feel OK with him being part of *her* thing?

"I don't have to stay here if you don't want me to." Tally doesn't notice Gory approaching and now he's standing a few feet away from her, the tiny kitten still in his arms. "I get it. This is your place."

Tally glances over at him. He isn't looking at her, his gaze firmly centred on the wriggling bundle of fur that he is holding as gently as if it was an actual baby.

"I like you, Tally." He strokes the kitten's head with his finger. "You don't look at me like I'm the most annoying person on the planet, and you're not always telling me that I talk too much. I don't have to pretend that I'm the same as you. I can just be me."

It is not what Tally is expecting to hear and the words swirl around her head. She knows all about people looking at her like she's different and acting like her different is somehow not right.

Maybe she was wrong. Maybe she does know Gory, just like she knows Layla and Jade. He's just another kid, after all – trying to figure out where he's supposed to be going when everyone else seems to have the map and they

242

aren't prepared to share it with you.

Well, this is her group. No – it's *their* group and they have got their own map. And she doesn't know where it's going to lead them, but at least they can all go there together. And Jade is right. In their group, everyone is welcome.

"He loves you," she says, leaning over Gory's shoulder. "You should give him a name. I think he looks like he should be called Cuddles or Whiskers or maybe Smokey, because of his grey fur."

Gory grins up at her. "I've already given him a name," he tells her. "Meet Hulk 2."

Tally frowns. "What? You can't call him—" Then she stops and takes a deep breath. Everyone should be allowed to voice their own opinion. Even if that opinion *is* a little bit ridiculous and it's not like the first Hulk is even dead, which would make more sense, and whoever heard of a cat called Hulk 2?

"Hi, Hulk 2," she whispers, reaching out and stroking his back. His fur is smooth and silky and so, so soft against her skin. "You are a beautiful kitten."

"Does that mean that I can stay?" asks Gory as they walk back to where the others are gathered around the box of baby chicks that Jack has brought outside.

"If you want to," says Tally. "But perhaps try to be a bit quieter because sometimes loud noises make me jump and I don't like lots of shouting, OK?"

Gory nods seriously. "My sister is autistic," he tells her. "But she's not the same as you. She can't talk very much, so I have to be quiet and listen really carefully when she wants to tell me something."

"How did you know that I'm autistic?" asks Tally. "Did someone tell you?"

Gory shrugs. "Nobody tells me anything. I just thought you might be."

Tally nods. It's exactly what she's been starting to think. Perhaps everyone is very different but a little bit similar at the same time. And maybe all the little similarities add up to something bigger than the differences between them.

Date: Wednesday 17th June.

Situation: Third day of camp.

Anxiety rating: 10 when I was accused of stealing the letters, which lowered to an 8 when Layla and Jade stood up for me. Then a 6 when Mr Kennedy gave me the choice of going home but I decided to stay, and finally a 3 when I was at the Sanctuary. I can't believe that I've managed to get to an anxiety rating of 3 when I'm away from home AND the day started so badly! Maybe Mrs Jarman was right when she said that we were all going to learn new things about ourselves.

Dear Diary,

Well that started out as the most horrible, awful day ever. My worst fears came true. I was publicly humiliated and accused in front of everyone and it was something I didn't even do. I don't know if I will ever be able to forget that moment. It was like an actual hot pain going through me, like someone was sticking knives in me. I mean I can actually take a lot of things, but even a firm tone of voice from an adult makes me feel dizzy like I'm going to faint.

So imagine how devastating it was to be shouted at like that, even though I did my best not to show the pain. Luckily it all ended up OK and at least they apologised. But even if I had done something wrong, that is absolutely not the best way to get me to behave better. It just sends me into a panic and stops me trusting that teacher. Gaining trust for an adult is so important; it's that which leads to me respecting them. Fear and respect are totally different things. Take Mrs Jarman, I really trust and respect her, because I feel I get the same back from her. When I left her those top tips in the first term, telling her how to be a better teacher for kids like me, she really took the time to listen and learn. It made a massive difference to how I felt about her lessons. Maybe one day I should make a factsheet for ALL the teachers in the school and give it to them. I don't quite feel brave enough to do it yet, but when I do these things will be on it:

Tally's Factsheet for teachers – THE TOP TEN THINGS YOU NEED TO KNOW ABOUT MY AUTISM AND DEMAND AVOIDANCE.

Understand that I often cover up my anxiety, and although I may appear calm and fine on the outside, this does not mean I am actually feeling it inside. I have learnt to cover my real feelings at school as I want to fit in and not get into trouble. It's hard to hold your real feelings in and pretend to be something you aren't all day. Home is the only place where I feel I can let my real feelings out.

Building a good relationship with me is the best way to help me feel calm and be able to behave and be my best. Show me that you like me by smiling and connecting with me positively when you see me. Like everyone else, I respond really well to feeling liked. Please try not to criticise me or say negative things to me as that will definitely make me feel that you don't like me.

Tone of voice and facial expression are really important to me as I read a lot more into them than other people might do. If you have to tell me off, please do it in a calm way, rather than in a cross or harsh voice. Please don't make sudden loud noises like shouting at me, as this makes me anxious. Sarcasm and criticism make my anxiety levels go sky high. Using nice language puts me at ease and will help me to focus on what you are actually saying rather than how it's making me feel.

Please, please, please, I beg of you, don't punish me by doing anything that shames me in front of other people, like detentions, making me stand up in front of others, telling me off in public. This is my worst nightmare and it is my biggest fear in school. It doesn't make me learn to behave better as I will be so anxious that I'm bound to do more things wrong. Please just speak quietly to me on a one-to-one basis. I absolutely promise I will take in what you are saying better that way.

Ask me to do things calmly and pleasantly and try not to make it sound like a command as this instantly escalates my anxiety – eg, "Would you mind coming up with a good way to make sure you remember your pencil tomorrow?" This is a good way to phrase things for me.

Don't ask me lots of direct questions as these feel like demands and the pressure can be really stressful. Say things like: "Would you be happy to share your thoughts?"; "I'm wondering whether you..."; "I notice that..." ; "I was thinking you could..."

Give me time when asking me questions or when giving me instructions. Don't get impatient with me or I will sense it and will be flooded with stress which makes it even harder to think straight.

Don't ask me to make eye contact as a way of showing I am listening – it makes it harder for me to listen. If you really want me to be listening carefully to what you are saying then let me look wherever I need to so I can concentrate.

Please don't force me into anything I do not feel ready or comfortable doing. I'm always pushing myself out of my comfort zone, but I can only do it when I feel in control. I will usually give most things a try when I feel ready to. Give me some control by offering choices; this always makes me feel more relaxed and motivated.

Most of all, PLEASE try to put yourself in my shoes and know that I don't choose to be this much work – this might be annoying for you but believe me it is ten squillion times harder for me.

CHAPTER 14

For the first time since she arrived at GoCamp, Tally wakes up with a sense of excitement. Sitting up, she gives a sleepy-looking Jade a wave and then looks across at the empty bed on the other side of the room. There has been no sign of Skye since yesterday, but the rumour around the camp is that somebody saw her getting into her parents' car. Tally has debated whether she should be feeling sorry for her, but has decided that, on reflection, her energy is probably better used elsewhere.

"It's the high ropes today!" she says as they start to get dressed. "I can't wait!"

Jade laughs quietly. "I don't think that Gory is as excited as you are. He told me yesterday that he's going to hide in the Sanctuary so that Kirsten can't find him."

Tally grins. "He'll be fine. We'll look after him."

Layla puts on her trainers and stands up. "I wish that I was in your group," she complains. "Team Basilisk has got dragon-boating today, but it'd be far more fun to be with all of you."

"At least you aren't in bottom place on the scoreboard," Lucy tells her. "Team Phoenix are not doing well. Kirsten says that we're the worst group that she's ever had."

"That's ridiculous," Ayesha tells her. "You're always on the winning team, Lucy. I thought you'd be in the lead for sure."

Lucy huffs. "I know, right? I'm always the best at sports, which is why it's so frustrating to be on a team with people who aren't sporty." She glances across the cabin to where Tally and Jade are standing. "No offence."

"None taken," says Jade, rolling her eyes at Tally the moment that Lucy looks away.

"But apparently it isn't our lack of skill that's holding us back," Lucy continues. "According to Kirsten we have '*no team spirit*' and we don't work to support each other. I don't know what she's on about, to be honest."

Tally sees Layla raise one eyebrow and has to busy herself tying up her laces so that Lucy doesn't see her trying not to laugh.

Outside the cabin, Gory is already waiting for them and they go together to the canteen where they grab some breakfast to eat out on the verandah.

"I'm dreading the high ropes," says Gory, pulling the crust of his toast. "I don't mind heights but I hate the way that ropes wobble about."

"We'll be right there with you," Jade tells him. "Just do what I'm going to do and pretend that you're a jungle cat, roaming the treetops with no fear."

Gory looks dubious. "Does that actually work though?"

Jade shrugs. "I have no idea. But it's got to be a better plan than sitting here getting all worried and scared about it."

"Has anyone seen Skye?" asks Layla. "She wasn't in our cabin last night but do you really think that she's been sent home?"

Tally shakes her head. "I don't know. Let's just be glad that she isn't here."

The bell rings signalling the end of breakfast and the doors to the canteen fly open, releasing the rest of the kids into the outside air.

"I suppose I'd better go and find the rest of Team Basilisk," Layla sighs, standing up and walking across to the steps. "Have fun on the high ropes!"

"We won't," groans Gory. "It's going to be a miracle if I survive this in one piece."

Tally laughs. "I'm pretty sure that we're all going to be attached to a harness and a rope," she tells him. "I watched a video of it with my drama teacher and she told me that there was no risk. She said that we might feel a bit scared, but that's totally not the same as being in actual danger."

Gory wrinkles his nose in disbelief and Tally pats his arm, the same way that Mrs Jarman did when she told her how frightened she was about falling off the high ropes.

It's another beautiful day. The sun is already high in the sky and there's a delicious smell of warm soil and salty sea air. As Tally strolls along the path, listening to the other two having an animated discussion about the wonderful world of cats, she suddenly feels a bubble of happiness explode in her head. She stops walking and stands completely still, soaking everything in. It feels so good to be right here, right now with these people.

This is the way life should be.

"Tally? Are you coming?" calls Jade from up ahead.

Tally grins and starts walking again, catching up with her and Gory as they reach the turning for the high ropes activity.

"Oh no," murmurs Gory, his face falling. "That's not good."

"It's all going to be fine," says Tally. "There's nothing to worry about."

"I'm not sure that's entirely true," gulps Jade and Tally looks in the direction that they are both staring in.

They were right. It's not good and there is definitely something to worry about. It is about four foot nine inches tall and has a lot of very blonde hair that is currently being swished over its shoulder as if it owns the place.

"I thought she got sent home?" whispers Jade.

"Well, she's here now," groans Gory. "Just when I thought that the high ropes couldn't get any worse. Can't we just leave? I've got a really brilliant place to show you and we could just go there?"

"We can't just walk off. And maybe she'll be a bit nicer now?" suggests Tally. "You know – now that everybody knows what she did?"

"Gather round, please!" calls Kirsten, approaching from the other side of the trees. "We'll just give you a safety briefing and then get you going. It's all mostly common sense – as long as you listen to what you're told and don't do anything daft, then everyone is going to have a fantastic morning high up in the treetops!"

"Well, that means Gregory is in trouble then," mutters Skye, managing to find the perfect volume that adults can never hear but all the kids do. "Mr Limpkin has been telling us all week that he hasn't got any common sense."

Tally glares at her but Skye has already turned away.

So much for hoping that she might have lost some of her bite.

Kirsten starts explaining the safety procedures and Tally listens carefully to the rules. She's not worried about the height of the activities, but she's feeling pretty nervous about having to balance up there with only a rope to protect her.

Kirsten finishes talking and the other two instructors start to hand out the harnesses. Ameet, Lucy and the two girls from Redhill High are put together and taken off to a different starting point, leaving Tally, Jade, Gory and Skye to form the other group.

"Good luck!" calls Lucy as she heads off into the trees.

"We're going to need it," mutters Tally, casting a glance at Skye.

"You need to put this on," says an instructor, handing Tally a harness. "Step in through the leg holes, like you're putting on a pair of shorts."

Beside her, Jade and Gory start to get ready. Skye

reluctantly accepts her harness too.

"Just so you know," she murmurs to Tally when the instructor has moved away, "I really don't like you."

Tally blinks and looks back at her, briefly lost for words. But then she remembers what Mum always says to her, whenever Tally is having a meltdown and yells the same kind of thing at Mum.

"That's a shame," she tells Skye. "I'm very sorry that you feel like that about me."

Skye's mouth drops open for a moment and curls into a snarl.

"You're playing a dangerous game if you think you can mess with me," she hisses. "I'm only here because my parents think that their cruise is more important than my happiness. I don't want to be here and I definitely do not want to see you. Stay out of my way."

"Gladly," Tally says. "We don't want you in our group either."

Skye narrows her eyes, but before she can say anything else, Kirsten beckons them across to her so that they can all be safety checked.

"Now, this isn't a timed activity," she tells them when they're all standing at the bottom of the first challenge. "The main aim of this morning is to put yourself out of your comfort zone and work together. You're going to start by climbing the wall and then, once you're at the top, you'll find instruction cards telling you what to do next." She pauses and gives them a big smile. "You'll follow the course right to the end and there will be instructors on the route, making sure that you're correctly clipped in to the ropes. There are points available for working well as a team, but the most important thing is to have fun! Now off you go!"

Tally looks at the others. Jade is shuffling from one foot to the other, looking nervous. Gory has gone pale and is muttering under his breath. Skye is standing slightly apart, with a look on her face that suggests she has smelt something disgusting. She might be wrong but it's hard to imagine that any fun is going to experienced this morning – or that they could possibly ever be a team. Not with Skye in their midst.

"Let's get it over with then," sniffs Skye, starting to pull herself up the climbing wall. "I suppose I'll need to take the lead."

Tally flings herself at the wall and quickly grabs a handhold. There's no way that she's going to let Skye boss them about and there's no way that she's going to let her think she's better than they are.

"Come on!" she yells to Jade and Gory who are still at the bottom. "Let's go!"

Not looking down, Tally climbs as fast as she can, but Skye still makes it to the top before her.

"What took you so long?" she drawls. "And what a surprise – your little friends are taking for ever." She sighs and casually inspects her nails. "God – we're going to be up here all day."

"You two can make a start on the next challenge," says the instructor who is standing at the top of the wall. "I'll just clip you in and then you can make your way over to the other side of the platform, where you'll find an instruction card."

He unclips them both from the climbing wall and moves them across to the next safety rail. Skye marches off and, after a moment of hesitation, Tally follows her. She wants to wait for Jade and Gory, but she can't bear for Skye to be in charge and do everything first.

"This one is so lame," complains Skye. "Although you and your loser friends will probably be terrified." She sneaks a look at Tally and wrinkles up her nose. "I've done far better high ropes activities than this. This place is pathetic. I mean, we're hardly even off the ground."

Tally looks down and then wishes that she hadn't.

The ground seems a very long way away. If she falls, she doesn't think that she'll be getting back up again.

But she can't let Skye see any of this.

"I'll go first," she says, pushing past Skye and reading the card. "We have to get across to the other side by standing on the tyres and holding on to the ropes."

"Easy," yawns Skye.

Tally ignores her and, holding tightly on to the first rope, steps out on to the dangling tyre, suspended high above the forest floor. The tyre sways and she clings to the rope, waiting for the movement to slow down so that she can stretch her foot out to reach the next one.

"In your own time," says Skye from the safety of the platform. "We've got all day."

"You're doing great, Tally!" calls Jade, and when Tally looks, she sees that she and Gory have made it to the top of the wall and joined Skye at the entrance to the tyre challenge.

The tyres swing and sway and it takes every bit of Tally's strength to cling on to the rope and not lose her balance. Finally, after what feels like for ever, she makes it across to the next platform.

"You're doing brilliantly!" she yells across to Jade, who is already partway across the tyres. "Well done!"

Jade keeps on coming, her footing slow but sure. She's breathing quickly by the time she reaches the platform but her face is lit up with a proud beam.

Tally gives her a high-five and then looks back out, wondering if Gory will be next. But it's Skye who is stepping out on to the first tyre and so she turns away. She has absolutely no interest in watching Skye make it across in record time and then having to listen to her brag about how easy it was.

"Skye's taking ages," says Jade. "Look. Do you think she's OK?"

Tally looks. Skye is standing very still in the middle of the tyres, and she can see from here that her fists are tightly clenched around the rope.

"I'm sure that she's fine," she shrugs. "She's probably stopped to figure out a few more nasty things to say to us when she gets over here."

"I don't know—" starts Jade but then Skye begins to move, stretching out her leg and quickly transferring her weight to the next tyre.

The instructor gives Gory the sign to start, and he steps tentatively on to the first tyre, moving slowly towards Skye.

"You can do it, Gory!" yells Tally.

"Just don't look down!" adds Jade, and Tally turns to

her, a frown on her face.

"You shouldn't say that to him," she tells Jade, her voice serious. "Now he's only going to want to look down. If someone tells me *not* to do something then I always *have* to do it."

"In that case, please don't stop talking," sneers Skye, coming up behind them.

Tally ignores her and turns her attention on to Gory, who is bravely making his way across the tyres, although she can tell by the look on his face that he hates every second.

"Were you OK out there?" Jade asks Skye. "It looked like it was a bit tricky when you got to the middle. It was scary, wasn't it?" She gulps. "I'm not sure how we're going to cope with the next challenge – I hope they don't get any harder."

"Scary?" sniffs Skye. "Are you serious? I got something in my eye and I had to try and blink it out. And I've got no idea how *you're* going to cope with the next challenge either – you couldn't have been any slower on the last one, Kitty."

Tally spins round.

"Call her that name one more time and you'll be sorry," she shouts. Jade puts her hand on Tally's arm, but she shakes it off and steps forward. "I mean it. She's my friend and I am not going to let you keep treating her like she isn't important."

Jade makes a small sound and Tally can feel the rage building in her body at the unfairness of it all. She swallows hard, trying to keep it down. Her hands start to flap at her sides and her legs start to jiggle and all she wants to do is close her eyes and put her hands over her ears and block everything out.

"What are you going to do?" taunts Skye. "Tell on me? Because that didn't exactly work out for you last time, did it?"

Jade puts her hand on Tally's arm again, and this time Tally lets herself be pulled back. Skye is right. Telling a teacher what happened with the letters didn't make any difference to her attitude. Maybe giving Skye a good, hard punch in the face would help though?

There is a sign pinned to the tree that is growing up through the middle of the platform. It reads: *Now You Can Get Closer To The Edge.*

Skye is pushing Tally closer to the edge than she's been in a long time, but she's fairly sure that the sign isn't talking about that.

"I'm not going to tell on you," Tally says, her voice

quiet. Her ability to keep her fear and confusion and anger reaches its limit and her hands start to stim.

She lets them.

"Good," says Skye. "Because we both know who the teachers would believe – and it isn't you. That's why I'm still here. Because they can't be sure that I actually did anything wrong, and my dad emailed Mr Limpkin and told him that if he sent me home without any evidence then he'd sue the school. He's a very successful lawyer and he always wins all his cases. There's no way Mr Limpkin is going to go up against my dad."

"But you had the letters in your swim bag," whispers Jade. "I know you did."

Skye shrugs. "Nobody can prove that it was me. Maybe you put them there to get back at me," she says.

"Move on!" calls Kirsten from below. "There's no time for chit-chat!"

Skye smirks nastily at them and moves around to the opening to the next challenge.

"I *didn't*," Jade whispers to Tally and Gory as they slowly follow her. "I'd never do something like that."

"I know you didn't," Tally reassures her, unclenching her fists and trying to calm down.

"Well, I wouldn't blame you if you did," huffs Gory.

"She's vile."

The next challenge involves stepping on pieces of wood that are hanging high above the ground, like tiny floating platforms. Gory volunteers to go first but he only gets as far as the second piece of wood before a wail floats across the treetops.

"I can't do it!" he cries. "I want to get down."

"Just hurry up," snaps Skye from behind Tally. "This is boring and I want to get it over with."

"You can do it, Gory," Tally says, leaning out from the safety rail. "Just look straight ahead and step across the gaps."

"I've been reading about the number of times a rope can be used before it's too frayed," he whimpers, clutching on to the rope. "How do we know how many times this rope has been used?"

Tally smiles. Finally, a problem that she can deal with. She knows the answer to this question because it was one of her worries before she came on the trip.

"They check the ropes every week," she calls to him. "And there's a log-book where they write down how many times each rope is used. It's completely safe, Gory."

"Do you promise?" he shouts back.

"Oh, for god's sake," mutters Skye. "This is ridiculous."

"I promise on Skye's life!" yells Tally. "You've got nothing to worry about."

Skye glares at Tally, but she doesn't care because Gory has started moving and is slowly and very shakily making his way across the wooden walkway. Jade follows him and then it's just Tally and Skye left.

"What have I ever done to you?" asks Tally, turning to look at Skye. "Why do you hate me so much?"

Skye opens her mouth as if she's about to say something, but then changes her mind. Tally watches as she steps out on to the first piece of wood and begins to make her way across the obstacle. The breeze picks up and the ropes start to swing. Skye stops in the middle, just like on the last challenge.

"I don't want to do it." The words are muffled by the wind, but Tally can still hear them. "It's stupid."

On the other platform, Jade and Gory hear them too.

"Just keep going!" calls Jade. "You can do it!"

"No!" yells Skye. "The walkway is broken and I'm not carrying on. This is a really stupid task."

"I did it!" yells Gory. "I did it and I was super-scared, so if I can do it then you totally can, Skye! You're way braver than me."

He isn't trying to rub his own success in Skye's face.

He's trying to help, although Tally thinks that he really doesn't understand anything if he truly thinks that Skye is braver than he is.

"Someone get me down!" screeches Skye. "This activity is stupid!"

"You need to work as a team." Kirsten's voice floats up from far below. "Skye needs you to go out and help her across the course."

Tally folds her arms and leans back against the tree truck that goes right through the middle of the platform. If it were Jade or Gory out there then she'd think that they were frightened, but it isn't them. It's Skye and Tally is fairly sure that this is all just a ploy to get some attention.

"Please?" Skye's voice is quieter now. "Please help me."

On the other platform, Tally sees Jade and Gory look at each other, their eyes widening as they hear a sound that it's almost impossible to believe is real.

Skye is crying.

"I'll come across!" Gory shouts to Skye. "Just hold on tight and I'll be with you in a minute."

"No way!" Tally steps forward and calls across to her friends. "You shouldn't have to go back out there just for her."

"We can't just leave her there," protests Jade, waving

her arms in the air. "She's scared."

We can totally leave her there, thinks Tally, although she manages to keep the words from escaping her mouth.

"I can do it," calls Gory, bravely. "I don't mind."

Tally frowns. He does mind, she knows that. He's loathing every single second of this activity and it's absolutely not fair for him to have to go back out on to the walkway for someone as horrid as Skye.

"I'll go," she shouts. "I've got to get across anyway so it makes more sense if it's me."

"If you're sure?" Gory's face floods with relief.

Tally nods and then, holding firmly on to the rope, steps out on to the first piece of wood. It wobbles beneath her feet and she tightens her grip, trying not to think about how far it is to the ground below. Taking tiny steps, she shuffles forward until she's at the edge of the wood and then, holding her breath, steps across the gap and on to the next piece.

"I'm coming," she calls to Skye. "Just hold on."

The next piece of wood is smaller than the last and Tally can feel her heart pounding in her chest. She reminds herself that she's perfectly safe and that nobody has ever died at GoCamp and that the very worst thing that can happen right now is that she falls off and has to be lowered down to the ground by her rope. The problem with this kind of thinking is that her brain doesn't really care about the whole *rope* part of the situation and can only focus on how terrifying it would feel to fall from here.

But she keeps going and, finally, she reaches Skye, who is standing very still with her eyes firmly closed.

"You're not going to fall," Tally tells her, seeing Skye's shaking hands. "Just take a deep breath in and then let it all out. Then do it again."

Skye's eyes stay closed but she does as Tally says and takes several deep breaths.

"How are you feeling now?" asks Tally after the third breath.

"I'm still stuck out here on this stupid challenge," mumbles Skye. "How do you think I'm feeling?"

"OK." Tally frowns. "Well, the only way to get down is to either let them lower you on the rope or walk across the planks to the other platform. Which one do you want to do?"

Skye's mouth twists into a snarl. "There's no way that I'm letting them lower me down," she hisses. "Are you *crazy*?"

Tally scowls. "Do you want my help or not?" she snaps. "Because you don't really deserve it."

"I'm sorry." The words are so faint that Tally has to lean closer to hear them. "I do want you to help me."

"Fine." Tally shifts her balance so that her feet are further apart. "But first you have to promise to never call Jade any name that isn't her own, actual name and you also have to promise never to use *that* word again."

"What word?" Skye sounds confused.

"The *crazy* word," Tally tells her. "I'm autistic, not crazy. When you call someone crazy you're making them feel small and unimportant and useless and it's not OK."

"I won't say it again," promises Skye.

"And while you're at it, you can stop making fun of us. The things that you laugh at me and Jade for are part of us being autistic."

Tally knows that this probably isn't the best time to have this particular conversation but she might not get the chance again and it's been upsetting her all week, hearing the way Skye and her friends are so unkind whenever someone does anything that they think is stupid. "I'm autistic, not *wrong* – and it's hurtful when you act like we're something negative. It makes people think we're no good at anything and that's not true."

"I get it," huffs Skye. "Now can we get off this thing?"

As apologies go, it isn't the most impressive that Tally

has ever heard, but as the floating walkway has started to sway quite alarmingly she supposes that it'll have to do. She's out here now and if she wants to get across to the other platform then she's going to have to find a way to make Skye calm down.

"I'm coming across!" yells Gory, and when Tally looks over, he is tentatively starting the return journey back towards them. She thinks he's pretty brave to even *think* about doing such a thing for someone as mean as Skye, but she's glad to have some back-up. Maybe the two of them together can come up with a plan.

"Please help me," murmurs Skye. "I'm frightened."

Tally blinks and stares at the other girl. She has said quite a few surprising things since they all arrived at GoCamp, but this is the most unexpected of all.

"OK." Tally nods her head. "I know all about being scared and I can totally help you get across to the platform, but you have to do exactly as I say."

She tightens her grip on the rope and tries not to look down. Skye isn't the only one who could do with a few calming techniques right now.

"I'll do whatever you want," whimpers Skye. "Just hurry up."

"If we're going to create a relaxed feeling then we can't

rush it," Tally tells Skye. "Now, I want you to imagine that you're in a place that makes you feel happy. Somewhere safe and relaxing."

"What do you mean?" asks Skye, opening one eye and squinting at Tally. "What place?"

"Well, for me it's somewhere high up," Tally tells her. "I like to imagine myself lying in a hammock in the treetops or floating on a cloud, far away from everybody else and with the whole world spread out beneath me."

Skye shudders and Tally realizes her mistake.

"But *you* could imagine somewhere low down," she rushes on. "Like a cave or a tunnel or maybe a dark cellar. That's probably the kind of place that someone like you would love."

"What's the point of this, exactly?" asks Skye, opening both eyes now. "Are you trying to freak me out even more?"

The wind gusts again and the dangling pieces of wood shift. Skye's knuckles go white as she clings on to the rope and Tally sighs. Skye is making it difficult to help her and it would be so easy just to turn back and leave her out here on her own.

"OK, I'm here," pants Gory, finally making it to the walkway on the other side of Skye. "What's the plan?"

Tally shrugs. "I haven't got one. I tried to get her to

think about her favourite place but she hasn't got one. I'm all out of ideas."

Gory holds on to the rope and looks at Skye. "It's not very far to the platform," he tells her. "You've made it this far so you can totally get over there."

Skye turns her head slightly and looks at him. "Do you really think so?" she whispers.

He nods and slowly manoeuvres himself so that his back is to the girls and he's facing the platform where Jade is waving encouragingly.

"You can do it!" she yells.

"I can't believe this is happening to me," moans Skye. "Even Kitty managed to do it and—"

"That's enough!" roars Tally. "I *told* you that I'd only help you if you agreed never to call her that again and you've broken your promise. I've had enough of standing out here waiting for you to decide to move – now turn around and follow Gory!"

"I can't—" starts Skye but Tally ignores her, grabs hold of the rope and puts her foot on to the piece of wood where Skye is balancing.

"You can!" she insists. "Hold on with your hands and look at Gory. Do what he's doing unless you want me to overtake you and leave you out here on your own. Now, move!"

And Skye moves. She reaches out and grabs hold of the next piece of rope and starts to shuffle across the plank, only hesitating when she reaches the edge.

"I'm counting to four and then I'm going to squeeze past you," Tally warns her. "One, two—"

"I'm going!" squeals Skye, launching herself across the gap. "Just stop having a go at me, OK? You're being horrible."

She throws herself at the next plank and then the next and Tally follows hot on her heels, determined not to let her stop and cause yet more fuss.

"You did it!" cries Jade, when they're all on the platform. "You helped Skye get across! We all made it!"

"I wouldn't say that we helped her, exactly," mumbles Tally, glancing anxiously across at the instructors. There's a strange sensation seeping into her cheeks and she realizes that she feels ashamed of how she's treated Skye. Skye was scared and Tally knows she probably made things worse.

"What are you on about?" asks Gory. "You're the one who got her moving again. You completely helped her."

"I doubt that she sees it that way," Tally tells him, watching as Skye dabs at her eyes and then follows the instructor towards the escape ladder. "I wasn't very kind."

"Great job out there," says Kirsten, who has climbed

up to meet them. "Excellent team spirit! Now, Skye has decided that she'd prefer to give the last few challenges a miss but are you all still up for doing them?"

Tally looks at Jade and Gory. Neither of them was looking forward to this task and Gory in particular was terrified about the final death slide challenge.

"I don't mind if you want to stop now," she tells them. "I'll do whatever you want to do."

Jade looks at Gory. He gulps slightly.

"I thought I'd be petrified about doing this," he admits. "And it's true – I was. I still am. I hate heights and I'm scared of falling and I keep wondering what would happen if there is a freak hailstorm while we're up here because I saw something about that in the news. But I think that I can do it if you guys are doing it with me, because it doesn't seem as scary when there's more than one of you, although that probably makes no logical sense because the more of us that there are, the more potential there is for disaster." He hesitates and looks at them, his face a bit red. "Is that OK?"

Tally grins at him. "It is definitely OK," she tells him. "And everything is less frightening when there's more than one of you. That's just the way it works."

CHAPTER 15

They can hear the thudding sound of the beat way before they reach the doors to the Centre. Tally grimaces and clenches her fists. The last-night disco is supposed to be a treat and everyone else is really excited. Cabin One totally stank of body spray by the time Lucy, Ayesha and Layla had finished getting ready, and Tally had to put her head under her duvet to breathe in any air that didn't make her feel like she was about to choke to death.

"They're playing my favourite song!" says Layla. "Come on! I want to dance!"

Tally drops back so that she's next to Jade.

"Do you like this kind of thing?" she whispers as the three other girls race up the steps.

"I don't think so," Jade whispers back. "I think I'd rather be reading a book, if I'm perfectly honest. Music isn't really my thing."

"Hurry up!" calls Layla, bouncing up and down. "The chorus is the best bit!"

She's right. Tally loves this song too and she can never hear the chorus without wanting to move her feet. Music really *is* her thing – she can't imagine a world without melodies and harmonies and steady, pulsing beats. She just likes being able to choose what she listens to and when she listens to it, and she knows exactly the volume that she wants to hear her favourite songs being played at.

And the deafening noise flooding out through the open doors is definitely not the correct volume.

But Layla loves discos and Tally wants to be a good friend.

"Shall we just go in for a little bit?" she asks Jade.

Jade nods and together they follow Layla inside. Everyone is huddled against the walls and the middle of the floor is completely empty.

"Why is nobody dancing?" asks Jade as they make their way towards the far corner where Gory is standing on his own, looking distinctly uncomfortable.

"They don't," Tally tells her. "Nobody ever dances at a school disco. Haven't you been to one before?"

Jade shakes her head. "Why would I do that? It's

bad enough having to go to school every single day. I'm not exactly keen to put myself through more trauma in the evening."

Tally nods. She understands how it feels to need your own space. Right now, she'd do anything to get out of this room with its bright, flashing lights and overwhelming noise. It's taking every bit of strength that she possesses not to slam her hands over her ears and curl up in a ball on the floor.

"Hey!" shouts Gory as they approach him. "I'm so glad that you guys are here!"

Layla grins at him and gives him a thumbs-up.

"I just wish people would dance!" she shouts back. "It'd be way more fun than standing around talking."

Gory nods his agreement and they start talking animatedly about the best songs to dance to. Tally and Jade find a space against the wall and lean next to each other.

"We could just stay for five minutes and then leave," Jade suggests, seeing Tally close her eyes. "It *is* very loud in here."

They stand there quietly for a couple of minutes and then the music starts to fade out and Mr Kennedy's voice booms out of the loudspeaker system.

"OK!" he shouts. "We'll be announcing the winners

of the Best Team Award and also the Best Cabin Award at the end of the evening. But for now, let's play another song. It's an oldie but a goody, and I'd like to see as many of you as possible out on the dance floor, showing us your funky moves!"

Everyone groans. The music comes on and Gory turns to look at them all, his eyes sparkling.

"I love this song!" he calls. "My dad plays it all the time because it makes my sister happy and we have to dance for her every time she hears it."

He pauses and Tally can see that he's tapping one foot.

"I can't *not* dance to this song!" he shouts. "It's the rule in our family. I have to do it!"

So, right there in front of everyone, Gory starts dancing. He lifts his legs and waves his arms and moves to the beat, a huge grin spread across his face.

Everyone stares. Absolutely everyone. And it would be wonderful to say that they are staring because they can't believe that he has a previously undiscovered talent for dance, but Tally knows that isn't true. They're staring because he's doing something different.

They're staring because he's *Gory*.

Her heart starts to pound in her chest and next to her, Jade clutches her hand. The music picks up pace and

Gory's wild movements propel him out into the middle of the room, his arms flailing and his feet pounding the floor.

"What is he doing?" calls a voice. "Is that supposed to be dancing? What a loser."

"I have no idea," yells someone else. "Whatever it is, he's rubbish at it."

Tally has to agree. He *is* rubbish at dancing.

But he isn't doing it to be the best or to get praise or to be a winner. He isn't even doing it for himself. He's doing it for his sister, because it's what he does to make her smile.

But nobody cares about that. They aren't interested in Gory or his story or who he really is. They don't know him.

Laughter starts to spread around the canteen, quietly at first and then increasing in volume until it's almost as loud as the music. Gory falters for a second, his eyes darting across the room to where a group of kids from his school are pointing and jeering. Tally watches as his smile drops and his arms go still and she knows that he's seconds away from giving up.

Her feet are acting before she can even think about stopping them. One foot in front of the other, racing across the floor until she's standing right in front of him.

"Let's dance," she says and then, as the chorus kicks in

she starts to move. Gory stares at her for a moment and then he is back in his zone, waving his hands in the air and wiggling his hips. Tally isn't sure when Layla and Jade join them. All she knows is that the four of them are together on the dance floor, grinning and giggling and not caring what anybody else thinks. And it's true – none of them are going to be winning any awards for best dancer of the night, but that's not why they're doing it. Gory is doing it for his sister and the rest of them are doing it for Gory.

And it feels so, so good.

The music ends and flows instantly into another song. The four of them pause and glance around the room. Somehow, without them noticing, other people have joined them and the floor is filled with laughing, dancing kids. Nobody is looking at them any more. They're all just having fun.

Gory blinks hard and pushes his hair back out of his eyes.

"I have to go somewhere," he says abruptly, and before they can stop him he's gone, dashing across the room to where the teachers and instructors are standing. They see him grab hold of Jack's arm and say something to him. Jack nods and they both disappear out through the door.

"Do you think he's OK?" asks Tally. "Maybe we should

go after him."

"He probably just wanted to have some time with Hulk 2," says Jade. "He's not on his own. Jack will look after him."

Layla lurches forward as someone crashes into her from behind. "Do you want to keep dancing?" she asks Tally, glaring at a group of boys whose dancing resembles something that might be seen on a rugby pitch.

Tally shakes her head. "No. I'm going to go outside where it's a bit quieter."

"I'll join you," Jade tells her. "My first school disco has been *quite* fun but I'm ready for it to be over now."

"You can stay though," Tally says to Layla, gesturing to the other side of the room where Lucy and Ayesha are dancing.

Layla smiles. "I'm good to go," she says. "It's getting really hot in here and I don't even like this song."

Tally isn't sure that's entirely true but she doesn't say anything. She doesn't want to stay in here for another minute and she doesn't mind if Layla stays without her, but she can't pretend that it doesn't make her feel warm and fuzzy and happy inside that Layla would rather be with her.

"That was amazing dancing, Tally!" Aleksandra sways

over to where they're standing. "And look – you got every-one else dancing too!"

"What can we say?" says Jade, casually. "We're trend-setters. Everyone wants to be like us."

Tally and Layla burst out laughing and Jade smiles shyly, her cheeks reddening with pleasure.

"It's really good to see you," says Tally, giving Aleksan-dra a quick hug. "Maybe we can sit together on the bus tomorrow?"

Aleksandra beams. "I'd love that," she tells her. "We've got loads to talk about and I've missed you this week!"

They smile at each other and then Layla gestures towards the exit. Tally looks at Aleksandra, who nods, and together, the four girls push their way through the throng towards the doors and the cool, quiet night-time air.

"I can't believe we're going home tomorrow," says Jade, leaning on the rail that surrounds the verandah. "I'm looking forward to seeing my mum but I'm going to miss all of you."

Tally smiles. She's been imagining what it's going to feel like to be back with Rupert tomorrow and she cannot wait.

They walk across to the outside table and sit down. The next hour is filled with chatter and catching up and a lot of laughing as Aleksandra tells them horror stories about sleeping in the tent. The night gets darker and Tally rubs her arms, feeling the chilly air against her skin.

"Hey!" A figure emerges out of the trees and waves his arms. "Do you want to see something brilliant?"

Layla laughs. "He's been asking us that for days. Do you think we should just go and get it over with?"

Tally nods and the three girls climb down the steps and head across to where Gory is standing.

"What is it then?" asks Jade. "And is it far? Because I don't really like the dark and I don't think we're supposed to go off without a teacher."

Gory grins at them. "It isn't far," he assures them. "And Jack knows what we're doing so it's all fine. Now *come on*!"

He leads them back towards the trees and then, instead of taking the path that heads down to the bay, turns left. The girls glance at each other but follow him. In front of them is another, smaller path leading steeply up through the wood.

"I haven't seen this path before," says Layla. "What's up here?"

Gory ignores her question and races ahead. "Hurry up!" he calls. "You're so slow!"

"I'm going to turn back in a minute if he keeps on being

so bossy," pants Tally, as they climb further upwards. "I'm going as fast as I can and my legs are tired and it's dark and I can't see anything and, oh!"

They have broken out of the trees and are standing at the edge of a wide, flat expanse of grass. And there, over by the edge of the cliff, shimmering and shining in the dark night, is the biggest swing that Tally has ever seen, lit up with hundreds of tiny, twinkling fairy lights. She can hear the sea crashing on to the rocks at the bottom of the cliff, and it's the most perfect scene that she could ever have imagined.

Tally blinks, just to make sure that she really *isn't* just imagining it. But it's absolutely and unmistakably there. And so is Gory, grinning from ear to ear as he sees the looks on their faces.

"Isn't it amazing?" he says. "I told you it was something brilliant!"

"Did *you* do this?" asks Tally.

"Well, I didn't make the swing," says Gory. "But I did put the lights on, with a tiny bit of help from Jack. That's what I've been doing for the last hour."

"It's beautiful," Tally tells him. "But why?"

He looks down at the ground and shuffles his feet before answering, suddenly shy. "My sister loves fairy lights," he mutters. "I had the idea of putting them on here when we were all dancing to her song. I thought you might like them – it was probably a stupid plan."

Tally doesn't know why, but her throat suddenly feels like she's swallowed a marble and her eyes feel all prickly, as if she's got something in them.

"I don't think it's stupid," she says quietly. "I think it's wonderful."

"How did you find it?" asks Jade. "I didn't even know this place existed."

Gory grins. "I was just exploring," he tells them. "That first day when we got here. It's why I was late for the raft-building challenge."

"But why is the swing even here?" asks Layla. "It looks huge – I reckon we could all fit on it easily."

"I'll show you why it's here," says Gory. "Get on it and you'll see."

They walk across the grass and sit down on the swing. Gory and Layla sit on either end and Tally and Jade squeeze into the middle. It's a tight fit but once they shuffle up a bit, it's cosy and snug.

"Now we all have to push with our feet," Gory instructs. "Three, two, one – push!"

Four pairs of feet shove hard on the ground, propelling themselves backwards. Four sets of legs drive the swing forwards and backwards. Four pairs of eyes gaze at the sight that awaits them when the swing reaches its zenith and three mouths gasp as they see the sea spread out beneath them, with a few glittering lights bobbing up and down on the water from the boats that are moored near to the cliff.

The fourth mouth doesn't gasp. Gory has seen it before. Instead he laughs with pleasure at the reaction that his surprise is getting.

As they swing back and forth, Tally feels like she is flying, with the whole world at their feet.

"This is the best," she whispers, reaching out and giving Gory's hand the quickest of squeezes. "Thank you."

"Thank *you*," he whispers back. "I was dreading this trip but it's actually been OK. Kind of."

She nods and looks back out to sea. He's right. Some parts of the week have been great and some have been terrible, which when you balance out probably does equal *kind-of-OK*.

"I wish we'd found this place sooner," says Jade, as they continue to swing.

"Excuse me!" huffs Gory. "I *did* find it sooner. If you'd listened to me then you could have been coming here every day."

"We should have listened to you," agrees Jade. "I will make sure that I absolutely listen to you from now on."

"Does that mean that you're going to keep on talking to me when we get back to school?" he asks.

"Are you going to keep talking to *me*?" counters Jade. "Because I'm either Cat Girl or the Invisible Woman in year seven."

Gory shakes his head, looking confused. "Don't be daft. You can't be invisible if we can see you. And you weren't invisible when we were dancing, were you? None of us were."

"More's the pity," mutters Jade, making Tally snort with laughter. "OK – so we're going to hang out together when we get back then?"

"Absolutely," says Gory. "Everything is going to be great!"

Tally knows that this is not how it always works. But as she listens to Jade and Gory talking about their plans to start a Cat Appreciation Society at Redhill High, she thinks that maybe, their story might have a happy ending. Or at least a hopeful ending, which is almost as good.

She leans back in the seat and tilts back her head. The fairy lights are glimmering against the dark sky and she thinks that she has never felt happier or more peaceful than she does right now, swinging in the darkness with the sounds of the sea in her ears and her friends all around her.

Discovering this place on the last night is absolutely perfect.

Date: Thursday 18th June.

Situation: Last night at camp.

Anxiety rating: Right now, it's a 2. I know – I can hardly believe it either! Sitting on the swing, listening to the waves at the bottom of the cliff was totally incredible and it's like the longer I sat there, the lighter my head became. All the worries and upset and hurt of the week just swung themselves right out of my head and all that mattered was being there, in that moment, with my friends.

Dear Diary,

Friends are the most important thing in the world, after Rupert and my family, obviously. Sometimes I mess up my friendships by getting too possessive because I feel worried about losing them. Sometimes I make friends with people who don't really understand me – and that usually ends up going wrong. But even though I've had some pretty horrible experiences with other people, it has never stopped me wanting to have friends. People some-times think autistic kids don't want friends, but they're wrong – or they are in my case, anyway, and Jade's too. I love having friends – it's what gets me to school in the morning. No, having friends is not the issue for me – it's making them in the first place, which is hideous. And sometimes keeping them. So you know what's coming next, don't you? Yep, it's another "Tally Adams tells you all you need to know" section coming up right here...

Tally's tips for friendship:

My mum told me once that some people are radiators and some people are drains. It took me a long time to work out what she was going on about, but now I know. Always try to be friends with the radiators. These are the people who bring you warmth and make you happy. Don't waste time on the drains, who suck your energy away. Those people can choose other friends who are right for them – you should always choose who *you* want to be with and not just wait around to be chosen by people that might not be a good match for you. Be careful that you don't jump into a bad friendship just because you are thankful that this person is showing interest in you. You never have to be grateful for someone wanting to be friends with you, because you are an amazing person. Yes, you are. You just might need to remind yourself about that sometimes, like I do. And definitely NEVER stick around with people who give you a bad feeling.

When you meet someone you just aren't sure about,

let your brain and heart debate and decide if that person is right for you. What I mean by that is use your instinct as well as your cleverness to help you decide. People might think autistic people don't have an instinct for things, but I think we can have an even better instinct than most. For example, I can just sense when something is wrong or a person isn't going to be good friend material. The problem is that there's a big difference between *knowing* something and *listening* to that knowledge. It's easy to get caught up in the moment and ignore that inner feeling, when you are looking for new friends and hoping that this person will somehow turn out to be nice. Hope is a great emotion at times, but it can also get in the way of your instinct. You can't rush into finding those real friends who are really there for you and you can't force friendship to appear. When it happens, it happens,

But when you find your true friends you will know because suddenly you will be having real fun with people who make the effort to properly understand you. It feels like you're safe, because you know that there will always be someone who has your back, no matter what. Bullies mean nothing when you're all in it together. It's true that together you are stronger. Never ever forget that.

And having a tribe of your people means that you don't

have to pretend. You don't have to say that you're OK when you aren't, and you don't have to act as if you think something is great when you don't actually like it. And you can be yourself. Like, I told the others about how sometimes I still watch Peppa Pig and we ended up having a massive conversation about which episode is the best one and it was really fun. And it's not just me that feels like this. It turns out that Gory had never told anyone about his sister being autistic because he thought they'd be unkind. I still don't know why he told us that day, but I'm glad that he did (he chose the right people to tell, that's for sure!).

What I suppose I'm saying is that nobody is on their own, no matter how much it can feel that way sometimes. Even on the days when you feel invisible and misunderstood, there is always someone out there who can see you; someone who knows you and understands what it's like to be you. You just have to look for them. And if you can find those people and make them your friends then everything will end up working out better than you ever thought it would.

Everything will be OK.

CHAPTER 16

The coach pulls into the school car park. Tally leans across Aleksandra and peers out of the window. It seems strange to be back at school, when so much has happened this week. She's worked so hard all week to fit in but the closer she gets to home, the harder it seems to be to keep a lid on everything. She feels like a volcano that everybody thinks is dormant but that really, under the surface, is bubbling away, ready to explode.

But Tally can't see much out of the grimy window, and so she sits back in her seat and tries to keep her feet from jiggling while she waits for the coach to stop.

"Have a great rest of the weekend," says Layla, from across the aisle. "I can't believe we've got to come to school on Monday morning."

Tally smiles at her. She can't think about Monday right

now. The only thing she can think about is going home to Rupert.

"I can see my mum standing by her car," calls Aleksandra. "Excellent! She's terrible at being on time and I thought that I might have to wait for her."

"I hope *my* mum waits for me inside the car," moans Lucy from the seat in front of Tally. "It'll be so embarrassing if she's standing there when we get off the coach."

"Totally embarrassing," agrees Ayesha. "I told my mum that I could walk home on my own but she insisted that she was coming to collect me."

"I hate it when people make a fuss when we get back from a trip," says Lucy, flicking her hair so that some of it flies thought the gap between the seats. "I'm like, honestly – how old are you? Five?"

"Can you see my mum?" Tally asks Aleksandra quietly. "Did she come with your mum again?"

Aleksandra squints out of the window, craning her neck to peer between the dirt that is splattered against the glass.

"I can't see her," she tells Tally. "She's not with my mum so she probably came separately."

Tally shuffles from side to side. She hates the scratchy, velvety fabric that the coach seats are made from and she regrets wearing shorts today.

"I can see my mum!" shouts Ayesha, her sudden yell making Tally jump. "Mum! Mum! I'm here! I'm back!"

She bangs on the window as the coach turns off its engine and Miss Perkins stands up.

"Right then," she begins. "We're going to get off in an orderly and—"

Tally doesn't hear the rest of the sentence because suddenly, everyone is out of their seats and racing down the aisle. Layla grabs her hand and pulls her and, with Aleksandra behind her, she is carried, like a leaf in a stream, down the coach and out into the bright sunshine.

"Mum!" screeches Lucy, not sounding *that* embarrassed to see her mother waiting for her. "I've missed you *so* much! I was completely homesick every night and I didn't sleep a wink."

Layla grins at Tally, who smiles back. Lucy slept really well every single night, and they know this because her snores kept the rest of them awake for hours. Not that they'd ever tell her that.

"See you on Monday," Layla says, spotting her Mum waving at her.

"See you on Monday," Tally replies. All around her, kids are reuniting with their parents and collecting their luggage and loading up cars and the air is filled with noise and excitement and chaos.

And then she sees them. Mum and Dad, standing by the wall. Waiting for her. Their faces light up as they spot her and then Tally sees Mum take a step forward, her arms folded across her chest, which is what she always does when she's worried about something.

Tally's heart clenches and she rushes towards them. Something is wrong.

"What happened?" she calls. "Tell me."

"You're home!" cries Mum, opening her arms. "How was it, sweetheart?"

"What's going on?" demands Tally, screeching to a halt. "It's something bad, isn't it?"

"I don't know what you mean," says Dad, his face wrinkling. "How was the trip? Did you get on OK?"

Tally stamps her foot in frustration. "I know that you're both worried about something," she shouts. "Don't try to pretend that you aren't. Is it Rupert? Have you let something terrible happen to him?"

Mum shakes her head. "Nothing has happened to him," she says gently. "Take a deep breath and try to calm down."

Mum has obviously completely forgotten everything that she knows about how to help Tally feel calm, because telling her to calm down is absolutely not a tactic that works.

"You folded your arms across your chest," Tally snaps. "And Dad's face is all wrinkly. Plus you're both staring at me in a really odd way and these are all the things that you do when you're nervous or anxious about something." She pauses and takes a deep breath, but not because Mum told her to do it. Just because she needs to breathe. "So tell me what it is that you're worried about, OK?"

Mum looks at her.

"*You*," she tells her. "We've been worried about you being on the trip. There's nothing wrong with Rupert – in fact, Nell is waiting with him outside the school gates because we thought—"

Tally is off before the words are fully out of Mum's mouth. She races down the path, dodging suitcases and parents and other kids, and then finally rounding the corner. And there is Nell, looking as bored as she possibly can, leaning against the gate and holding on to a lead. And at the end of that lead is Rupert.

He sees Tally before Nell does, which means that

Nell very nearly ends up flat on the floor as he bounds up towards his girl. Tally drops to her knees and pulls him to her, burying her face in his fur and holding him close.

"I've missed you so much," she tells him. "I've missed you the most of all."

"Well that's charming," mutters Nell. "I've missed you too, little sister."

"I'm sure that Tally has missed us all *just* as much as she's missed Rupert," Dad says, as he and Mum come up behind them with Tally's bright, purple bag dangling between them. Tally doesn't want to hurt anyone's feelings when she's only just got home so she keeps her head down and doesn't contradict him, snuggling up to Rupert, who shows her just how pleased he is to see her by licking her knees.

"Let's get you home, shall we?" suggests Dad.

"Mum made your favourite cake to welcome you back," Nell tells her as they walk to the car. "It looks amazing. Feel free to go away again any time."

"Don't you want me to be home?" asks Tally. "That's not very nice."

"No! That's not what I meant." Nell starts to roll her eyes but then stops, which Tally is glad about because she's told her time and again that the eye-rolling thing makes her feel horrible. "I meant that if Mum only makes cake when you've been away that maybe you should go away more often because—"

She pauses as Tally puts her hands on her hips and glares at her.

"It was supposed to be a joke," she offers. "I'm glad that you're home. It's been too quiet without you. And I've missed you."

"I suppose I might have missed you too," Tally says. "A little bit. And that was a rubbish joke, but the way. My friend Gory tells rubbish jokes too and I pretend to laugh to make him feel better, but you don't need me to make you feel better so I'm not going to pretend."

"I *always* need you to make me feel better," Nell tells her as they climb into the car. "But I don't ever want you to pretend."

Mum starts the engine and they pull off, leaving school behind. Tally stares out of the window and looks at the familiar sights as they flash by. She's only been gone for five days but everything seems a bit different and a little bit shinier.

"So why were you worried about me?" she asks, as

Mum pulls into their drive. "You didn't need to be worried."

"Of course we were worried." Dad twists round in the passenger seat. "It sounded like you were having a dreadful time."

Tally frowns. "What are you on about? I mean, some of it was a bit tricky but I'm best friends with Layla again and I made some amazing new friends called Jade and Gory and I'm still friends with Aleksandra so that's a lot of friends if you think about it. And there was a fantastic place called the Sanctuary where we could help with the rescue animals and a giant swing that could swing you right over the sea and it was brilliant. And we didn't win the Best Team Award or even the Best Cabin Award but it doesn't matter because being the best isn't the most important thing."

She pauses for breath. Mum turns off the engine and turns to looks at her.

"It's just that your letters were quite, err, quite – how should I put it?"

"Quite miserable and depressing," interjects Nell. "You sounded like you hated every minute."

"Oh. That." Tally shrugs and opens the car door. "They were just letters. They didn't mean anything."

"Clearly," murmurs Dad. "I wish we'd known *that* over the last few days."

He goes round to the boot of the car to get her bag and Mum opens the front door.

"Would you like some cake now?" she asks Tally as they walk into the house. "Or would you rather get settled in first?"

"Cake now," mouths Nell behind Mum's back.

Tally isn't really hungry and what she really wants to do is go to her room and lie on her bed and not do anything for a really, really long time. She definitely doesn't want to have to sit and eat in front of other people and talk about the week she's just had.

"Here's your bag," says Dad, putting it on the hall floor. "I bet there's some smelly clothes in there after everything you've been up to."

It's the absolute worst thing that he could possibly say. *Smelly* is one of the many words that Tally has banned the family from using since she was a very little girl. It makes her feel physically sick because of how it sounds and what it means. She feels her fists tighten and her head start to pound and she spins round to face him.

"What did you say?" she hisses, through gritted teeth.

"Sorry, it just slipped out. I didn't mean that you—"
starts Dad but Tally has already turned away. She can
feel the tension bubbling up inside her and more than
anything else she doesn't want to spoil everything by
losing control right now. She knows that Dad is excited
that she's home, and in his excitement he's just *forgotten*. She sometimes forgets important things when she's
excited, too.

"I'm going in the garden," she mutters.

And then she walks through the kitchen, unlocks the
back door and heads straight out into the garden with
Rupert right behind her. She did it. She knew that a
meltdown was coming and she figured out a way to help
herself. Tally knows that it won't always work out this
way, but it did today, and that makes her feel pretty great
about herself.

Together, Tally and Rupert go down the path and
past the old tree, which hasn't got any fruit on it yet, but
Tally knows will be laden with apples in a few months'
time. They go right to the bottom of the garden and then
Rupert sits down at the foot of the ladder, knowing what's
coming next.

"I found some more people for our tribe," Tally tells

him, crouching down and stroking his head. "I know that we thought it was only us but actually, we were wrong. It's better if there's more than one of you and, no offence, Rupert – but you're a dog and you aren't much help to me when I'm out there in the world without you."

Rupert stares up at her and wags his tail, letting her know that he isn't offended in the slightest.

Tally pats him approvingly. "Good boy. Now, I know it can be hard when someone you like gets a new friend, but I promise you, they're going to *your* friend too, OK? You don't need to be jealous."

Rupert blinks his big eyes and settles down on his tummy. Tally knows that he'll wait at the bottom of the ladder for as long as she's up there. He would wait for her all night long if she didn't come down, she knows that. Sometimes she thinks that he'd wait for her for the rest of his life, but she tries not to think that thought very often because it makes her feel happy-sad and it's too confusing and difficult to feel more than one emotion at a time.

She puts one hand on the ladder and starts to go up. The first step reminds her of how brave Gory was when he clambered onto the raft. The second step makes her think about Jade encouraging her to climb up the rock face when she was frozen with fear. Step three, as she avoids the rotten third rung of the ladder, brings back the memory of Skye being so unkind but Layla standing up for her. She keeps on climbing and remembering and when she reaches the top, she carefully scales the roof until she's standing with one foot on either side of the ridge.

The world is spread out beneath her, magnificent and huge and a whole lot of work. And Tally Olivia Adams is *not* huge. She is one small girl and there's just so much that she has to do. And it's hard and it hurts and sometimes she wants to give up and crawl into bed and on those difficult days when she thinks that she *can't*, the only thing that she wants to do is hide.

But those days don't last for ever. And on the other days, the good days, it doesn't matter how small she is.

Because Tally Olivia Adams is tenacious and incredible and she *can*.

ACKNOWLEDGEMENTS

Rebecca would like to thank Adam, Zachary, Georgia and Reuben for always being happy to talk about bookish things and bringing her multiple of cups of tea when she is deep in the midst of writing.

Libby would like to thank her family for all the love and support they give her – Mum, Dad, Rosie, Henry, Emma and Andy. Special thanks to Jack for being a great extra big brother over the years and providing the inspiration behind the character of Jack in the story.

A big thank-you also to all the teachers who have been understanding, patient and supportive over the years, and continue to be. Extra gratitude to Mr Jackson, who was the best primary head teacher ever!

Finally, Libby would like to thank her school friends, old and new, for taking the time to know and see her for who she is – Ava, Ella, Poppy, Erin, Ellie, Brooke, Samantha, Mya, Cali, Eniz, Lexie, Lily, Izzi, Matilda and Layla. And to her oldest friends – thanks for always being there – Daniel, Lucy, Salim, Anis and Tess.

We would both like to thank Fiz Osborne and the whole Scholastic team for being so wonderful and bringing this whole project together; Julia Churchill for her fabulous support; Lizzie Huxley-Jones for another insightful sensitivity read and Polly & Elsie Couldrick and Wanda & Freya Wall for once again reading an early draft and sharing their thoughts.

ALSO AVAILABLE FROM LIBBY SCOTT AND REBECCA WESTCOTT

People think that because Tally's autistic, she doesn't realize what they're thinking, but Tally sees and hears – and notices – all of it. Endearing, insightful and warmly uplifting, this is a story of autism, empathy and kindness that will touch readers of all ages.